True Love

....

Tim B. Scout

Contents

1.Coincidence

☐ ▫▫▫▫ ▫▫▫▫

Everything's a good cause that happens and leads to something very beautiful yet eradicated.What a beautiful heaven we live and should be proud of whatever we have but I don't.

A display of solemn life reminds you of your past and it always has a say.

'Your past has its beauty yet no one finds to believe because your past holds the truth.'

It has a way of coming into your life and drawing you down.

Well, I have nothing to display over here because today my fucking step-mom thought to let me out after months of cleaning her cranky floors and peeling walls.

"Get your ass down you little fool or I'm not letting you out. " She screams from downstairs.

I look in the mirror scanning my outfit which was too revealing for a woman to go out at night.

She gave this dress to me and made me wear it even if I didn't want to. I walk downstairs feeling the eery stairs.

"Do you even know that we are already late and you're showing me your slutty dress? " I try to open my mouth but she shuts it down.

We sit inside a car that maybe she had booked. We drive out of the city. I open the windows feeling the fresh air after so long.

A little glimpse of redness surrounds the sky as it fades away, the darkness taking its place as the celestial objects make an appearance.

Natural light sources in the night sky as the moonlight cascades down. The light breeze flowing its way making my light curls flow.

The car comes to a halt as we come in front of a dark alley. I walk out of the car and see a club I snap my head back and look at my stepmother.

" Why are we here? " My voice cracks as I ask her.

" Shut your mouth and follow me inside. " She walks leaving no space but to follow her.

A dark luxurious club with a smell of drunkards. I walk inside before getting bumped into a hard rock.

"What the fu..." I looked at the person whom I had bumped.

My eyes as I look up the man standing before me. His face was carved by a Greek god.

I looked down at his body which was tensed yet he didn't show any rage or emotion.

His body was something that would put any woman on their knees. His hair slicked back. His beard was perfectly shaved. His sleeves rolled up where I could see his perfect veins.

The black slacks and dark dress shirt he wore only accentuated his tall, well-built frame.

"Fuck." I breathed as I looked at him only to realise my words.

His lips made way as a smirk landed on his lips

□□□□□□ □□□□□□.

Money doesn't decide your worth it's how you think to use it. Every penny has its words of hard work but you need more yet in a more easier way.

I don't have much to be descriptive about as I'm a hectic person with an egoistic temper. People shiver whenever they hear my name.

This day couldn't get worse when I bumped into someone. Already my day was going bad and now bumping. I'm going to kill the person who bumped into me.

My eyes wandered at the woman who looked at me.

My eyes directly went to her eyes which captivated me. She was gorgeous with a little dress which hugged her curves perfectly. The slit was just perfect to show her toned legs and her cleavage which was visible.

Something about her demeanour made me want to know more about her as I eyed her up to down.

"Fuck" I heard instead of a sorry as she realised her words which came out of her little plump lips.

She noticed as my lips carved into a deadly grin.

This woman seemed interesting to me as she hesitated and looked down fidgeting with little fingers.

I wanted to ask her more but a voice interrupted us.

Her eyes had turned dark as she heard the voice.

'Lily'

Her name was Lily.

As Lily turned to the voice calling her name, Zaeden couldn't help but notice the shift in her demeanour. The darkness that clouded her eyes intrigued him, adding a layer of mystery to her already captivating presence.

He watched as she hesitated for a moment before reluctantly making her way toward the source of the voice.

Curiosity piqued, Zaeden decided to follow her discreetly, his steps silent as he trailed behind her. The club was bustling with activity, the thumping music and dim lighting creating an atmosphere of secrecy and allure.

The voice came from a different way yet she went in another way ignoring the source.

As he observed Lily from a distance, he couldn't shake the feeling that there was more to her than met the eye.

Lily approached a table where a man was waiting, his features obscured by the shadows. Zaeden's instincts sharpened as he sensed tension in the air, a silent exchange unfolding between Lily and the mysterious man.

Their conversation was hushed, but Zaeden caught fragments of words - betrayal, consequences, and a dangerous game.

Intrigued by the unfolding drama, Zaeden made a decision. He would keep an eye on Lily, drawn to her enigmatic aura and the secrets she seemed to be hiding.

As the night progressed, he found himself entangled in a web of deceit and danger, his motives becoming intertwined with Lily's mysterious past.

"What the fuck are you doing here? " A woman asked holding her hair.

She dragged her around the club. "Sir, the woman has come. Would you like to meet her?" Rhyan asked Zaeden as he looked at the disappearing figure.

Zaeden wanted to decline the offer but it seemed that he had come far away to let the offer decline. He made his way towards the private room.

————

The chapters would be short at first but it gets better.

2.Strangers

□□□□ □□□□

She dragged me to the other side of the club as a hallway could be seen. My scalp hurt as she dragged me by my hair.

She entered a VIP room and a person was standing in the corner. There's so much darkness on the one side that I can just watch the leg.

Suddenly the door opened. I didn't budge from my place to see the person as he would be one of those motherfuckers which you can find in any corner of the world.

Something was wrong, I felt something bad was going to happen. The cool air in the room felt hot as nervous took my place.

My body shuddered as she came closer to me tilting her head towards my ear as she spoke."Behave."

The words lingered in my mind. The footsteps retracting could be heard but I paid no attention.

I huffed out as I looked around the dark room which displayed nothing but a couch on both sides of the mahogany desk.

" So as per the contract says." The guy standing at the side of a couch said. "Your daughter will be with us until you pay the handed money. "

My head snapped at the woman sitting beside me. I felt nauseous as the words felt heavy on me. She is selling me to a man that I don't even know and for money.

I felt disgusted at myself for being born into this hell.

This is where this was going to end right? I'm changing it.

I can't even stand up to her low-life instincts. We had enough money to have three meals a day and a nice maid I was. Tears pricked my eyes as it took place.

Betrayal.

Suddenly the man who was sitting in front of me came in the light. My breath hitched, and my heart started beating loudly. He was the same guy whom I had bumped outside.

This is not going to happen. I can't be with him looking at the big smile on his face tells me that he is a bad person. His existence is tensing me up.

Something about him is captivating but I don't want to get tangled in these things. As if my life was more than perfect this thing.

I know where this would end me being whore where he could fuck me however he wants and whenever and just for money. Why did he even bother to come and see her?

I don't even know the guy's name and she is selling me to a man because she took a loan from him and couldn't pay back.

I feel so strangled here as if anyone is not letting me breathe. I looked at the man as he was already looking at me. His gaze was making me hot already.

The woman beside me stood up as she went to sign the papers. I wanted to run away from here. I'm seeing my life taking a downstream here.

I can't let that happen, I can't let a man destroy my life.

I got up and came out of the room. The room started to throttle me in. My eyes wandered around the club before running to the exit.

I ran as fast as I could. I didn't know what area was it or what place.

She never left a second just to insult me and show me how I couldn't stand for myself. But it was enough and it was a limit where I could control myself.

Without looking behind I ran away. I don't even have money or anything. I'm just in this slutty dress.

I ran and ran till my breath ran out. I just saw some men in black coming in my direction so I turned and went into a dark alley.

"Wow!" I heard someone say as I walked. "What a young woman is doing here?" One of the men spoke coming closer to me.

" Hey don't come near me Or I would.... "

" You would do what? You can't even do anything such a beautiful art you are."

" Fuck off I'm not one of your women you bastards"

They started coming closer as I closed my eyes.

"No one would help you and we are not going to harm you. "

"What a sick bastards live in our society." I turned behind to the source of the voice.

"Wouldn't it be helpful for our country to remove the stain of you?" He spoke coming closer to us.

This man is such a beauty. Loose curls hang around his forehead. He's wearing casual clothes.

He waved his hand to come behind him as I went behind him. The perverts came forward to beat him but I think he's already good at defending and he did throw some punches around them.

As everyone ran away he looked back at me and smiled before coming towards me.

"Are you hurt somewhere? " He asked looking at me to see any bruises or injuries.

"Well I'm not but it looks like you are. " I replied as I looked at his bruised face.

"Oh, it's nothing this small bruise can't even do anything to me -ahh! " He screamed as I touched his face.

"I can see too. " I said as I suppressed a laugh. "Well it's your fault you touched before giving me heads up"

" Thanks... For your help " I thanked him.

"It's okay to help someone who is in need. Ummm... Hi I'm Chris "

"Hi. I'm Lily. It's nice to meet you, Chris. "

" You too Lily. Well don't worry about those guys I'll surely make them pay for their deeds."

"Thanks, Chris you did a lot for me. If you wouldn't have been here what might have happened."

"It's okay Lily no need to worry. It's what anyone would have done. "

"You helped me a lot today I can do a favour to you if you have."

His head snapped towards me as he thought about something and then said.

"Be my girlfriend Lily. "

———

3. A better place

□ □□□□□□ □□□□□□

"Don't run behind her. She will practically come to us."

She ran away from here and it was a bad decision to leave me with her pathetic mother.

The reaction on her face made a little step back for me. As if she didn't know her mother's wrongdoings.

The lady was borrowing money from us for her surgery but she had lied and in return she wanted her daughter to be taken.

The woman was begging to listen to her excuse and I was in the city and Rhyan told me that we should meet her.

Her daughter was..... Can't express it right now and I was willingly ready to keep her daughter.

'Lily.' Such a nice name she has but her intentions and attitude don't match her.

We moved out of the club and went to our house. I tied Lily's mom in the basement as my bodyguard came behind me "Sir we got her location and her Information too. "

I dialled Lily's number and she picked up.

"Hello"

"Don't you worry about your mother Lily"

"Who's this"

"Well, your mother begged us to meet her and I didn't know that she had such a beautiful woman and you just destroyed my plan."

"Well, you didn't have any consent of my willingness that I'm ready to come with you guys. I'm an adult and I can do whatever I want. "

"Then I don't have any option but to kill your mother."

"Kill that bitch she's not worth living "

A gunshot could be heard in the room.

"I'll send her body to you. "

"Oh, no worries Mister you can keep it as my gift to you. Thanks for killing her you helped me a lot. I was going to do it soon."

She hung up.

□□□□ □□□□

"Will you be my girlfriend?" Chris asked me.

I mean I couldn't say anything I was stunned at his sudden words.

"H.. I mean you need to pretend to be my girlfriend"

I sighed loudly when he completed his sentence.

"Is that bad being my girlfriend"

"No that's not what I meant, it's just that you suddenly asked me to be your girlfriend. "

"No worries, let me drop you home"

I looked down not able to speak after what happened. " I ran away " He looked at me and then took out his jacket and put it on my shoulder.

"That's a very gentleman"

"I was born to be gentlemen my lady" I laughed.

"It feels good "

"Okay, so you would be staying at my guest house and that's fine for you No buts. I'll pick you up in the evening tomorrow. "

I couldn't say anything and to repay him I can pretend to be his girlfriend right? That won't be much bad.

"So what's the special occasion? "

"Nothing much it's my parent's anniversary and I mistakenly said that I have a girlfriend and to prove to them I need to bring a girlfriend."

"Oh, not a long story"

He dropped me at his guest house and we exchanged our numbers.

NEXT day

It was 4 in the evening and I was drinking coffee when I got a call from Chris.

"Hey"

"Hi."

"Come down fast. "

"Wait what not now I'm not even ready Chris"

"Do you want me to come up and carry you? "

"No, I'm okay I'm coming right now "

I ran down leaving my state behind because I couldn't understand what was going on in his mind.

I was wearing my sweatpants with a beige crop top.

"Hey, can't you call me a bit earlier so I would have got ready? Look at me I'm looking like a homeless person right now. "I said huffing.

"You look beautiful in that state too Lily. " I blushed a little.

He drove the car and we reached Iowa very expensive shop of gowns and all

I went in first looking around the shop. It was so beautiful every gown and dress looked so gorgeous. lookeddress A lady came beside me and asked me.

"I'm sorry but we don't have anything that fits into your pocket."

"No, I ... " She didn't even let me complete the sentence.

"You have no place in here so get the fuck out.."

"She won't go anywhere miss. " He looked at her name batch. "Miss. Carry. "

"I think you need to leave from here. " I knew this was Chris.

"I'm sorry-. " He cut off her and spoke. " You're fired. "

"How can you disrespect my girlfriend just by looking at her clothes". He came closer to me and put his hand around my waist.

I looked at him as he winked his eyes at me.

" Choose whichever dress you like Lily. "

After like what felt like an eternity he liked a dress this dress was more comfortable for me.

I like this dress so much. It was comfortable and I didn't have the energy to change more dress.

We sat in the car after leaving the shop.

"Hey why did they bow to you at the shop earlier

"Do you know Relish Industries? "

"Yes, of course, I mean who doesn't know it "

"I'm the heir of Relish Industries"

"Ohh.Huh? What are you serious "

"Are you Chris Arden? "

"What do you think Lily?"

"That means I'm going to meet Mr Raphael Arden and Mrs Arden"

"Yes ma'am"

"No, I can't Chris that's not my thing"

"You can do it, I'm sure. ".

" Chris, why didn't you tell me earlier? "

" What should I tell you?"

"I mean anything how can I meet Mr. Raphael and Mrs. Arden. "

"It's okay just be cool and there's one more person you will meet. My brother would be there too. "

What the hell did I put myself Into? I hope this goes better.

————

Vote for the next story......

4. Endless Eternal

L ily Rose

I look at the mirror one more time before walking out of the room.

I look up to find Chris sitting down on the couch wearing a nice blue navy suit. His hair was slicked back, his beard nicely shaved.

He looks up at me and then at my attire. His mouth opens but there's no voice.

"Hey," I say walking towards him with my dress. "I don't have any words. You look glamorous. " He replies.

A blush crept into my cheeks. " Well, you look ravishing then," I say looking down at him. " So are you ready?"

I exhale a breath and then look at him. " Yes. " And he takes my hands and walks out saying. " Let's go."

At Chris place

My mouth wide open at the Mansion outside I see. Arden family has always been known for their Classic vintage style.

The car comes to a halt. I open the door and come out. I look around myself and feel more nervous.

His hand came around my waist and pulled me closer to him.

As we walked inside I was already mesmerized by the beauty of their house.

It was a vintage classic-style house.

"Be natural talk about yourself and just say you're my girlfriend."

I nodded. The doors opened revealing a family sitting on a large dining table.

Of course, Relish Industries is the second most billionaire company.

"Hi, son and you must be Lily, right? " A woman comes towards us clasping her hands together.

"Hi, mom. Happy anniversary to you guys " Chris wishes his mom as I go forward and wish her too.

"Happy anniversary to you ma'am"

"Oh Lily come on don't be formal with me you can call me Mom," Chris's mom says.

□□□... This feels good to someone who likes me at this instant.

She hugged Chris and me too. I feel like meeting my mom.

"Come on guys have a seat"

We sit at the dining table as Chris introduces me to his parents and they were so cute.

"So my eldest son is also coming and I want to introduce him to Lily too. "

"You have an elder brother too? "I asked Chris.

"I don't but it's like a business and family relation you can say. He's been with us since he was a teenager"

"Oh"

After chit-chatting with his family which felt like a real family.

"Chris your family is so cute. I already love them. Looking at your house I thought your parents must be vintage-style parents but they are so open-minded. I love them so much. "

Chris laughed at my sentence as suddenly his mother spoke.

"He's here, Lily Meet my son This is Zaeden, Zaeden this is Lily. She's Chris's girlfriend." Chris's mom says.

I turned around to look at the man standing behind us. My heart stopped beating when I saw him. He was the same guy from the Club whom I had bumped and my □□□□ □□□ was going to sell me to him.

My hold on Chris's hand tightened.

"Hey, are you okay? "

I looked at Chris and then at Zaeden as he was smirking... How can he smirk right now?

"Lily?" He shook me as I came out of my bewildered thought.

"Oh yeah I'm fine"

He pulled me towards him by my waist came closer to my ear and whispered.

"Don't be scared if you do something wrong you should be scared by me."

I pushed him by his chest and sat on my seat. Suddenly I felt two strong arms on my sensitive part of the waist.

I looked at Chris as he had a playful smirk.

"No don't do that you'd regret it, Chris"

He started tickling me under the table as I laughed.

"You guys make a very good couple. I hope you guys look forward to your relationship"

I looked at Chris as he was already smiling at me. But I felt a stare at me as I looked around and Zaeden was giving me a dangerous look.

I talked with Chris's mom as Chris, Zaeden and his dad were talking with each other. But still, I could feel Zaeden's eyes towards me.

I looked at him as our eyes locked together. I don't know why but I felt something in those eyes.

Feeling uneasy I excused myself to the restroom.

"You're okay, right? " Chris asks as I stand up from the chair. I nod my head and walk out of the room.

I don't even know where the washroom is. Maybe I would need a map.

Suddenly I heard footsteps coming around as I stood there until the footsteps stopped and I looked up.

My breath hitched as I saw Zaeden coming towards me I turned around and ran Inside a room.

Before I could do anything he turned me around and pinned me to the wall. "What the fuck are you doing? Leave me. " His grip on my neck tightened as he came closer to me making our faces just inches away.

"Is he your boyfriend Lily? " The first thing he asks is this?

"Why do you even care? " I say trying to wriggle out from his grip.

"Say it, Lily. Is he your boyfriend? " I rolled my eyes

"I knew it you guys were just pretending. He was never interested in having a girlfriend" He says loosening his grip on my neck.

"What if I am his girlfriend?" I say

He came closer to my ear. His hot breath touched my neck just to make me feel weak. He came to my neck, inhaling my scent. I felt something strange inside my stomach.

"I know you are not." He says and looks at my neck.

He suddenly started sucking my neck, I pushed him but he was way too strong and I gave in gaining pleasure from him.

"Zaeden... " I moaned out. He stopped and whispered in my ear.

"My name on your tongue spells so sweet." Before I could say anything He kissed me.

_____

Vote for next...

5.

L ily Rose

ROSE IVORY represents purity, charm, thoughtfulness and graceful-
ness and Independent.

My mom always said that I was her Rose ivory. Likewise, the word that is
used to represent my mom.

She always made me believe that she depended on me but I should never
depend on others I should be my own Rose Ivory.

My mom was the purest kind I could ever say. I don't have many memories
of her but the remaining ones I have are filled with laughter happiness,
madness and crazy.

She never made me cry or beg for anything.She made our family a whole
but she had a sickness and eventually died as her last words to me were.......

"□□□□ □□□□□".

I remember her still looking beautiful in her last breath as Dad held me.

I never cried in her last moments and showed all the love she gave me. I could never cry at that moment because she left us with love and affection that can never be replaced.

But right now I cannot be a ROSE IVORY.

Zaeden kissed me and I couldn't even control myself. His hot breath on my neck made me feel weak.

I gave in. He pulled me to himself as my hands went up to his neck for support. I can feel him smirk under our kiss.

Then I heard someone's footsteps coming near us.

I tapped Zaeden's shoulder to let me go but instead, he pulled me more and deepened the kiss. I started pushing him as the footsteps grew closer to us.

I pulled out and ran outside the room and tried to console my breath as I heard the footsteps stop.

"Hey Lily are you okay? I was worried that you weren't back. " I looked up to find Chris standing before me.

I

hear the door open and close behind me. I looked at Zaeden just to find him smirking. Is this man obsessed with smirking or what?

"Yeah, I'm fine it's just that your house is too big to find a restroom."

"I'm sorry for that. Let's go my parents must be waiting for you. "

Zaeden Carter

I don't know why but I felt good kissing her. An electric jolt dropped into my body as our lips touched.

She is good at these things. Might be good for one time.

If Chris didn't have interrupted us it might have...... "Let's go," He said to Lily as his hand went up to her waist pulled her closer and walked back towards the dining room.

My blood boiled. How can that bastard touch her?

I turned and walked to the balcony. I could see the Flower garden from here and my favourite flower is the Black Pearl Lily which symbolizes strength and resilience.

Strength is the ability to withstand pressure. Resilience is the ability to withstand adversity and bounce back from difficult life events.

My dad always made me believe that never have a weakness. You should be their weakness.

He wanted me to be the most dangerous ruthless mafia that you could ever think.

But to be a truthful mafia my first kill was to kill my mother. She was my weakness her pure soul and kindness was my half soul but my dad wanted no distraction so he made me kill my mother.

My mom's favourite flower was the black Pearl Lily. It's a white beautiful flower which had pearl-like black buds in between. That became my favourite thing

And now I might've found my real Lily.

What am I even thinking?

I walked back to the dining hall and I saw Lily and Chris whispering into each other's ear and Lily laughing. I don't know why but I don't like them together.

"Zaeden why are you standing there come here. "Chris's mom called me. I sat at my seat as I talked with Chris's mom but my eyes were still lingering on Lily.

She looked at me and our eyes got tangled into each other. " Lily you haven't eaten anything yet? Is it not good? "Chris's mom asked.

"It's just that I'm not feeling well. " She looks at me and then turns to look at Chris.

"Chris I'm not feeling well. Can you drop me home? "

"Yes of course ma'am" She glares at him.

"Mom I'm taking Lily to her house as she is tired" Chris said to his mom.

"Oh Lily it was lovely meeting you and I hope you will often drop by. "

"Of course Mom."

"It's nice hearing Mom from you. Oh gosh, I already like you so much."

"I'll take my leave. It was a very nice party and once again Happy anniversary. "

" Oh yeah thank you." They stand up as Chris holds her hand and helps her before they can walk out Chris's mom speaks.

"No wait you can't take Lily home right now. I'm sorry but Mr And Mrs Wilson are coming. You need to stay here for the meeting, as you know it's the most important one"

"Mom I'll be back soon"

"Your dad doesn't want any risk Chris and about Lily, Zaeden can drop her too. "Chris's mom looks at me as I smile.

"Yes of course Aunt you don't need to ask too. I'll drop Lily. "I said looking at her. Lily turned around to see me her face turned into rage.

"Thanks, buddy for the help. Lily, you didn't talk with Zaeden, right? You guys should introduce yourself in the drive. "

I looked at her just to see her face getting red.

"Mom I'll drop Lily outside"

Lily Rose

Chris held my hands and looked at me.

"You were the best one tonight. I had so much fun with you. My parents already like you so much. Lily, you're such a great person that I've met. "

As we were talking Zaeden pushed me and went towards the car.

'What a jerk'

"thank you for saving me that day, I don't know what might have happened if you weren't there."

" It's okay Lily take that as my gratitude.? I have arranged a flat for you and sent some money into your account"

"That was not necessary Chris"

"That's okay between friends"

"Don't you guys think that we need to leave for home" Zaeden said Interrupting us in the middle of our talk.

"Chris come here fast" His mom called him.

"I'm sorry Lily I'll call you at night. Bye... "

I was looking at his running figure when suddenly someone picked me up in bridal style......

_____

.

Vote for next part

6.

L ily Rose

I smiled at the disappearing figure of Chris and smiled at him. Suddenly I felt someone's hand at my waist but before I could do anything he lifted me in bridal style.

"The fuck. What are you doing? let me down Zaeden."

"You talk too much and waste time too. Shut up and get inside the car. " He says looking at me.

He looked at me with those dark eyes and my body felt weak under his stare. No Lily you are a.....

" If you let me down only I can sit inside your fucking car. " He walked towards his car.

He opened the door of the car and let me sit in the passenger seat. He came around and sat in the driving seat.

The awkwardness felt distant. I looked outside as it was dark. I couldn't see anything but suddenly the kiss scene came rushing into my head.

"Hey. Why did you kiss me?" I ask turning around him. Then he looks at me and smiles.

"Well, why did you kiss me back?" My throat goes dry as he asks me that question. I turn around and look outside the window.

"I asked first," I say looking out but he doesn't answer me.

I thought about the moments I shared with Chris. After a long time, I could see myself happy with his whole family.

I smiled. "Are you thinking about Chris"

I looked at him. He had an expressionless face.

My breath hitched when I felt Zaeden's cold but warm hand on my bare thigh.

'Oh fuck'

He stopped the car and looked at me. He came closer to me and whispered.

"Your house is right there up on the 11th floor and here are the keys "

'What? Is this man serious '

"Thanks for the help" I hope I never meet you again.

"You will meet me again Lily don't worry " He said.

I turned around and said "I hope I never meet you in my life you fucking moron. "

Third person pov.

As the sun dipped below the horizon, casting long shadows across the deserted street, Lily found herself standing face to face with Zaeden, a man whose dark aura seemed to blend seamlessly with the encroaching darkness. The air crackled with tension, their gazes locked in a silent battle of wills.

He came out of the car and went towards Lily.

Zaeden smirked, his eyes glinting with a malevolent spark. "You think you can outsmart me, Lily? You underestimate the power that lies within me."

Lily's jaw clenched, her resolve steeling against the palpable threat that emanated from Zaeden. "I know who you are, Zaeden. Your thirst for chaos will not go unchecked."

A faint smile played on Zaeden's lips as he took a step closer, the shadows dancing around him like malevolent spirits. "Oh, but you see, Lil cat, chaos is my domain. I was born to bring this world to its knees, to revel in the destruction that follows."

The night seemed to hold its breath, the tension between them thickening like a heavy fog. Lily raised her chin defiantly, her eyes flashing with determination.

"I will not let you destroy everything I hold dear. The light within me will always overcome the darkness that clouds your soul."

With a mocking laugh, Zaeden's form seemed to waver, his presence fading into the shadows that enveloped him. "We shall see, Lil cat. The game has only just begun, and in the shadows of deception, the truth may be the ultimate weapon."

As the echoes of his words lingered in the night air, Lily stood alone, the weight of their confrontation settling heavily on her shoulders. The battle between light and darkness had been reignited, and the shadows of deception threatened to consume everything in their path.

And so, as the night stretched on, whispers of a greater conflict stirred in the shadows, hinting at a destiny yet to be fulfilled. Lily knew that the road ahead would be fraught with challenges, but she also carried within her the unwavering belief that light would always triumph over darkness, no matter how deep the shadows may grow.

Lily Rose

His palpable threat lingered on my mind as I entered the apartment. The fragrance of a New house filled my nostrils as I took in the apartment.

I was apart from the dreadful part which had taken a part of me which I can never forget.

After changing into something comfortable I sat down on the couch.

My phone rang as I got a call from Chris.

"Hey"

"Hi Lily, I was feeling bit alone wanna join me for a walk"

"Yeah of course "

"I'm near your apartment. Come down fast" I walked downstairs as I saw him coming out of his car.

I went running towards him and hugged him. I needed a friend to share my moments.

We had so much fun it was meant to walk but we went to a game zone, ate ice cream and then had a walk.

Zaeden

Her words had caved away in my mind. Something was different about her. I don't know if it was her attitude or personality but she had this dark shadow behind her but it needed a way of looking to discover.

I left but I was still at her apartment's gate. I didn't know why but I couldn't leave something in me that wanted to wait for her. When I thought to leave I saw Lily coming out of her apartment and running.

I came out of my car and ran behind her but my heart stopped when I saw Lily and Chris hugging each other.

I turned back and went into my car.

I went home and had a cold shower.

I feel something with Lily that I don't feel with another woman.

This feeling of being with her is a new experience for me. I want to know more about her.

□□□□ □□ □□□ □□□□□ □□□□'□ □□□□□ □□□□□□ □□□□? ....

□□□□ □□□ Z□□□□□.

7. Lost

L ily Rose

Yesterday was the best day for me. Meeting His family made it even happier because after so long I felt like a family and at night meeting Chris made it even better.

We shared our happy moments and walked till we had a pain in our leg. It was so fun when he made a drama of having a cramp in his leg.

Oh gosh, he's such a dramatic person. But he's fun.

I think I came home at 1 maybe because we were too busy talking. I was so tired that I woke up at 11 am so close to noon. I need coffee right now to lose my tiredness.

I came out of my room rubbing my eyes and yawning walking towards the kitchen.

"Ahhh!!. "I saw Zaeden sitting on the couch and scrolling his phone as if it were his house.

"The fuck Zaeden. Why do you want to scare the shit? How do you come inside?" He didn't say anything and looked into his phone.

"You know that I can file a case on you for trespassing too? "

"Do you think you can case a file on me for trespassing? That's not funny to me Lily. " He looked at me from his phone.

He stood up and started coming closer to me as I started to back off.

My back touched the wall as he came closer to me till our bodies touched.

"Did you make me leave just because you wanted to meet Chris? "

Did he see us? Was he still waiting for me?

"Words Lily"

"Why do you even want to know that? What is it to you? "

He came closer to my ear as my breath hitched.

"You would regret that Lil Cat"

'Lil cat' that made my heart drop a beat.

I don't know why but I liked that nickname.

But realization hit me as he was so close to me, our lips were just inches away and our eyes locked to each other. His eyes were looking deep into me as if he knew everything about me. I looked at the side.

" I would never regret making you leave out of my house. I don't like you still you roam around near me like a creep. "

"Fine, I'm sorry Lily to make you feel uncomfortable. You would never see me again. " He said backing away. His voice sounded in pain.

"Wait! " I screamed running towards him as he turned around a little. " Where are you going? " I said lightly walking towards him.

But he still didn't move as he was still half facing to me. I heard his dark chuckle before he said."What it is to you? " He walked out.

A loud thump of guilt came into me when he turned around to leave. I stood there frozen.

'Should I stop him? I should stop him, right? He cannot leave.

But when I turned to stop him he was not there.

He left. He left. How can he leave me?

I felt something in my body. I felt weak. I don't know but I felt blurry. Things around me started to go in circles and eventually, darkness surrounded me.

□□ □□□ □□□□□□□□

I woke up still in a blurry surroundings. I rubbed my eyes to get a clear view. My head was paining like hell.

I saw Chris sitting on my beside as he called the doctor. I tried to sit up but my head was paining like hell.

"Chris... " I tried to sit up but he held my hand and made me lay on the bed.

"You're in the hospital. Lay down, the doctor's coming soon. " He said. Soon the doctor came and checked me.

"Now you're good Lily. You just had a small concussion. Just have a proper diet take the medications as per the given prescriptions and get a regular checkup. "

"Thank you, doctor" The doctor left as I turned to Chris.

"Did you bring me here? "

"Yaa... "

I felt heartbroken because in the last Zaeden was with me. How can he leave me in that state, does he not care about me?

But suddenly Zaeden entered the room.

"No, actually It was him who brought you here. He suddenly called me and said that you had fainted and were going to hospital. So I came. "

"But what was he doing at your house in the morning? " Chris asked.

I looked at Zaeden as he was already looking at me. But he didn't have any expressions.

"Lily had left something in the car so I went to give it back. " He said looking at me.

He came near Chris gave the medicines and handed him a file.

"These are her medicines and her reports. She hasn't been eating well and needs a proper rest and well nutrient diet. " He said looking through the file and secretly glancing at me.

He turned around to leave when I stopped him.

"Zaeden? " He turned to look at me.

"Thanks for bringing me here. " He turned around to leave again.

"Hey, where are you going? " Chris asked him.

"I'm going on a long business trip " He looked at me and said.

"For how long? "

"Don't know. I have some work with some of my other branches too. "

"What? " I asked

"Wait. Are you serious? " Chris asked too.

"Yes."

"For how many days? "

"I don't know maybe for a year or a two. "

What he meant when he said he's never going to me again.

" Best of luck with your new adventure Zaeden," Chris said.

"Thanks. I'll take the leave" He glanced at me and left.

He left. He left again leaving me alone.

In the whole conversation, his eyes never left mine.

Why did he have to leave me like that? After all that happened.

Did he feel bad about my words or my behaviour? Did it hurt him?

□□□□□□□ □□□ □□ □ □□□: □□ □□□□□ □'□ □□□□□□ □□□□□□. □□□ □'□ □ □□□□□□ □□□ □□□□ □□□□□□□ □□□□□□ □□.

8.

L ily Rose

After getting discharged, Chris helped me a lot and made me eat so many vegetables

He took a nice care of me. He's a good friend but the most I miss is...

'ZAEDEN'

I don't know but him being near me is something. I don't know but he never left my mind some way or other I was being reminded of him.

......

"Lily have your medicine and then get a proper rest. I'll come back in the evening to check on you. "

"Where are you going? " I asked him giving a sad pout.

"Cute but I have a meeting today that won't be long. "

"Okay, "He left.

'I don't have anything to do right now. Oh! I remembered that I have to apply for a job application.'

I got up and opened my laptop to apply for a job application.

Finally, I applied for a job which was suitable for my taste. And I applied for the billionaire company called 'Carter'.

I don't have much hope because that's a billionaire company and till now I don't have any experience. But I'll keep a hope.

Anyway, I'm gonna watch a movie right now.

□□□□□ □□□□ □□□□

I was getting bored so I checked on my phone and saw I had gotten an email from a company I clicked on the page as I got to know that..........

I was selected.

Oh, my gosh......

I called Chris to tell him the happy news.

"Hey Chris guess what? "I said being excited.

"Are you okay? "

"I'm super fine. I got selected. "

"For what? "

" I applied for a company and I got selected. " I jumped in the air.

"What" He screamed.

"Oh gosh. You are screaming in my ear "

"You should have told me Lily of course I would have helped you. Like you can ask me right? You know that na. Why didn't you tell me? I could have given you a job. "

"Hey, breathe. I believe you of course but I wanted something else on my will I wanted to do the things. I believe you Chris and you're the first one I would call."

"Fine but still. Anyway, I'm coming home soon. We have our celebration night remaining "

"Of course"

.....

□□□□□ □ □□□□□.

It's been a month that I haven't seen him yet. A part of me still misses him but my other half denies it.

But Chris was always with me. We went to movies, shopping, chilling, camping oh gosh I don't even remember the things now too.

I even started going to the office. It's a very chic classic but a high-class company.

It's one of the No. 1 billionaire companies. I still cannot believe that they accepted me. I mean did they make any mistake?

And to think of it, I got a new experience.

......

In the following week, I met Chris's mom too. She wanted to meet me and wanted to go shopping. So we went shopping as Chris was there to carry our bags. I should have clicked a picture of him it was so good.

It was fun meeting her. I didn't know that she would be so much fun.

I had a good with her. It was nice meeting her. She's a true meaning of motherly friend. I like her.

....

Today it might be a fun day because our company is holding a meeting with our clients in a club.

I dressed well. I wore a mid-length body con dress that hugged my curves perfectly with light makeup.

After the meeting, we all planned to stay back at the club so we could have some fun.

I got to the club. I went inside to was stunned by its beauty. This place is super deluxe man... I cannot complain about this.

I walked inside and I met with my colleagues and friends.

"Do you know that this club is funded by our company?" One of my colleagues said.

"Noo... I didn't know that " I said.

"Today our CEO of the company is joining us in the meeting too. " Other said.

"What??. "

Yeah I heard his super handsome "

"Guys we still have our meeting left and you guys are already drunken in our CEO's beauty whom you guys have never met. " I said.

"Lily you don't know but he's handsome".

" Okay, I believe that let's go back to the meeting before our CEO kicks us out for being late. " I said being sarcastic.

In the meeting room, I didn't see any CEO or something. Maybe he didn't come.

After the meeting, we all came out swaying our hips so eager to enjoy the free club.

I'm so happy to come back to the club. I once went to the club when I was in high school.

We had some Tequila Rose shots that were the best shot I have ever had. That was bitter in the first shots but it wr got sweet as the drink passed out throat.

We moved to the dance floor and danced. When I felt a person behind me.

I turned around and I met one of my colleagues 'Josh'. Everyone told me that he had a crush on me but I never minded that.

"Hey, Lily. "

"Hi Josh," I said still dancing.

"Wanna dance with me? " He asked.

"I'm dancing. "

"No, just with me "

"I'm dancing with everyone and you should join us too. "

"Please have a dance with me " He grabbed my hand.

"Josh I'm sorry but I'm gonna enjoy this night with everyone. " I said jerking my hand away.

I felt creepiness when his facial expressions changed a bit. We danced and drank till we got our knees weakened.

I sat feeling my legs giving out when one of my friends said something.

"Guys I'm going to the restroom. " I nodded at her as she went away. Suddenly Josh came and sat beside me.

"Lily, can you do a favour for me? " He asked me. I couldn't avoid his favour as I saw his face.

"Of course Josh " He took my hands and pulled me into a dark corner.

"Josh, can you leave my hands? " I said regretting my thoughts. He pinned me to the wall and said. " Lily I like you so much "

He said making my eyes go wide. I did know about this but the timing and place are not good. I knew this but I didn't know it was real. I thought they might be kidding with me.

"And you don't seem to show any emotions to my words Lily" He said coming closer to me. His eyes have changed and they seem to look darker.

"Josh can you move away I think I need to use a restroom. " I tried pushing him but he didn't budge.

" Lily can't you understand that I like you and I want to date and marry you? " I looked at him in shock. Marry?

"What?...... I'm sorry Josh I don't like you I only see you as a friend. " I said trying to walk out from his hold. "People always say that but don't mean it-"

"I mean it and I do like someone else and I'm waiting for him to come," I said in a bit rude tone.

"Were you waiting for me Lil cat? "

'Lil cat'

I turned around to the source of the voice.

Vote for the next part

9. ~~Losing Myself~~

L ily Rose

'Lil cat'

The dark husky voice that made me shiver ran down my spine.

He came back.

I turned to see but couldn't as it was a dark corner.

"Lil cat what the fuck is even that? that's too cheap don't you think lily. Who calls like that? And please it's between us, you should leave then Mr. " Josh said the last part to the person.

"Josh leave me, this is the last chance I'm giving you or else I'll call some-one-" He cut me off before I could say anything.

"What will you do? I like you Lily so much. why can't you understand? I've been dropping hints for you too. But you seemed uninterested. Come to me Lily I can give you the best life." I tried to push him.

"Josh this is getting too much. And you're drunk too, stop this and I'll leave." I said pushing him more.

He pulled me close and started coming closer when I felt someone pushing.

I fell on my hard chest as I looked up to see Zaeden standing there and looking at Josh with a deadly glare. I pushed him and stood on my legs.

He went to Josh and choked his throat. "How can you touch her with your filthy hands bastard? She is mine and don't ever think of coming closer to her. " He said as he was choking him hard.

"Leave him Zaeden. You will kill him" He glared at me.

I pushed him hard as he stumbled back. I ran to Josh who was breathing heavily.

I patted Josh's back to help him to breathe.

"Why are you helping him, Lily? Leave him and let's go" Zaeden said holding my hand.

"After you did this how can I leave him here? " I said jerking my hand back. "Lily don't be a fool. "

Without saying anything I got up and picked Josh's hand to help him but he jerked my hand got up on his own and left without saying anything.

I was going to run behind him but got pinned on the wall.

"The fuck -" Before I could say anything he came closer to me.

His hand roamed towards my waist and pulled me towards him.

My breath hitched our lips were inches away. His heavy breath on my neck. I looked at his eyes and then his lips and again his eyes.

"Triangle method huh!! " He said. I looked at his dark grey eyes which were cold and emotionless.

"Can you leave me? I need to go. I said looking somewhere else. His hand came up to my chin making me look into his eyes.

"Whom do you like and whom are you waiting for Lily? "

My eyes widened as I realized his words as those were the words which I spoke to Josh.

I tried breaking from his hold but no help.

"Let me go Zaeden. "

"Don't move " I didn't listen to him.

I tried but suddenly he started sucking my neck. He sucked hard as I still tried to push him.

He sucked hard as I tried to control my moans. He suddenly bit my neck.

"Ahh," I moaned. As he moved his mouth from my neck and looked at me and then at my neck.

"Finally. I can say that you're mine." He said and went out of the room.

I ran to the washroom and looked in the mirror just to get a reflection of my fresh red hickey which was visible.

I tried rubbing it but it wasn't getting off. Finally, I asked a lady for help as she gave me her makeup and said.

"Looks like your boyfriend bit too hard". She said as blood rushed to my cheeks.

I wanted to tell her that it was not my boyfriend but what could I even say?

'Who is he? What he is to me? Do we have any relationship? '

I left the washroom and went into the club. I asked one of my colleagues.

"Have you seen Josh anywhere? " She denied it.

I wanted to apologize for the behaviour and tell him that I didn't like him. But he was already gone.

It was past midnight and already I was feeling tired and all this shit happening.

Bidding my colleagues I came out from the club and started looking for a cab but there wasn't any.

Then a car came and stood in front of me I backed off. My hand went towards my back pocket to pull my......When suddenly the car's door opened and revealed the person.

Zaeden came out and asked me. "Come on I'll drop you ".

" Thanks but I'm okay. I can go on my own. "

I opened my phone to call Chris to pick me up when suddenly Zaeden came towards me picked me up and put me on his shoulder.

"What the fu- " I said.

"You're too stubborn. Can't you listen once? " And he spanked me.

"Hey," I said as blood rushed to my cheeks. "You're too stubborn. If you speak one more time I'll do that again. "

He came near his car and opened the passenger seat door opened.

I sat without saying anything. He came around and sat and looked at me.

I looked at him but suddenly he came near me too and put on the seat belt and went back.

I breathed and looked outside as he started driving his car.

I looked at him as his eyes were on the road but then my eyes fell on something.

It was his arm which was veiny and muscled. Oh fuck that was so sexy but my eyes fell on something else.

Lil cat was written on his arm. But it was small. He tattooed my nickname on his arm.

My hands went to his arm as I roamed my fingers on the tattoo.

He looked at me, his dark grey orbs which were cold were now soft but for a few seconds.

He again looked at the road and started driving.

"Did you tattoo my nickname? " I asked him.

He didn't say anything and rolled his sleeves down.

I chuckled lightly." That might be temporary or some other women's you have given them right?" I said sarcastically.

He stopped the car and looked dead into my eyes. His eyes were getting black. He was angry. He came closer to me and made me look into his eyes.

"Don't ever compare yourself with other women. Lil cat is your name only not others and this is not temporary. "

He pulled up his sleeves to show me. His hands came and took my hands into him and touched his tattoo.

I felt a shiver run down my spine touching his tattoo. Our eyes locked as my hands touched his tattoo, I felt some kind of connection. I pulled my hand back and looked outside the window.

My heart was racing at that time that it might blast anytime. I don't know how much time passed as he stared at me but I was already feeling nervous.

He sighed and started driving again. When we came near my apartment he slowed down the speed. I looked at him as his eyes were on the road.

When we reached my apartment he stopped and looked at me. Feeling nervous I looked at him. He might leave again and not come back. So not to regret I looked at him for the last time.

His dark grey eyes which I like the most were trying to say something but not being able to read.

"Thanks for the ride. " I turned around to get out of the car when he held my hand.

"Wait." I looked at him but he didn't say anything. Feeling pressured I pulled my hand back.

" I need to leave Chris must be waiting." Suddenly his eyes turned dark and cold. His breath is uneven. He was angry.

" Does Chris live with you? " He said in his dark husky voice.

I nodded.

"Ye. Yes after I fainted Chris wanted to move in with me just for 1 and a half months. " I stutter. Fuck how can I stutter in this moment?

"Go home, "He says his voice cold. "What?" I ask unsure of his words. "Home, Lily."

He said leaving me alone on the stranded path.

Vote for the next part.

10.IMPRÈVISIBLE

L ily Rose

"Go home. " He said and left. He didn't even ask me how I was. Not that I wanted him to and when I turned around to see. But he had already left.

I went home and rang the bell as Chris opened the door giving me a warm smile.

" Hey, how was your party? Did you have fun? " Chris asked.

As I remembered the whole scene that happened at the party. No, if I tell him he will be sad and angry and ask who is it, better I'll keep it my way.

"Yeah, it was really fun. The meeting was boring but anyway, we had fun. " Suddenly Chris got a call and he excused himself and went to the balcony.

I got changed and came to the living room. I went and sat beside Chris. " There's a surprise for you. " He said.

"What? "

"It's on its way"

"Are you ordering food from outside because I'm already full from dancing for so long and the alcohol that's been down my throat?"

"No it's something else." the doorbell rang.

" Look it's here" He said and waved me to open the door.

Feeling excited I went to open the door. Just to see my excitement fade away.

He was there standing before me.

"Zaeden " I whispered out. My mouth went dry.

Why was he here when he told me to leave?

"Do I have to stand here all night? " He said pulling me out of my thoughts.

I opened the door to let him inside. As he went near Chris.

"Hey, buddy. How are you? long time no see man. " They hugged after all they hadn't met for a long time and what did I get instead of a hickey?

My eyes widened as I ran towards the bathroom and checked my neck. I had makeup on it.

I was still standing at the door feeling nervous.

"Hey, you guys must have missed each other. " Chris said looking at me.

Me! missing him that's ridiculous

"Zaeden told me that you guys have also become close because he helped you to find the restroom and you invited him to your house but you fainted and all that happened, "Chris said.

I looked at Zaeden as he was staring at me and he was smirking oh gosh what is he thinking right now?

" And he called me saying that he was back so I invited him over to your place. "

So this was his plan. Does he think of me as less? No, now I'm going to make feel bad for his decisions.

Zaeden carter

'We live together ' that made me even more angrier. Are they couples NO so why are they staying together?

Feeling furious I called Chris.

"Hey, buddy. Where are you?" He asked me.

" I'm back," I said with a cold tone.

" So where are you staying right now?" He asked.

"I just came back. Maybe I'm going to my house, oh I can't I haven't told them I'm coming so yeah maybe at a hotel. " I lied.

" Come to Lily's house. I'm staying there. We'll have some fun"

"Why are you staying at her house? " I asked.

"Ohh after she fainted the doctor to care of her properly so I'm staying with her for a few days I'm going back tomorrow, she's well now. " I smiled at his answer.

"Okay I'm coming "

Looking at her stunned face is so good. I can fuck her with that face too.

Wait what am I thinking?

"Wait I'll bring water for him" She said and went to the kitchen.

I sat on the couch as Chris sat too. She came with a water of glass and gave it to me. I purposely touched her hand as she pulled it back.

Chris got on the left side of the couch and waved Lily to sit in the middle.

She looked at me and sat in the middle.

"Okay does anyone have a suggestion for a movie? " Chris asked looking at the TV.

Lily put her hands on his shoulder and whispered something in his ear.

He looked at her and smiled. He put on horror movies. Does it look like I'm afraid of these children's play movies? They don't scare me.

I have killed thousands of people but this is nothing to me.

The movie starts with Chris off the lights. Lily went closer to Chris as she might have felt scared.

But this made me more angrier.

Chris stopped the movie at the interval as he stood up and said

"I'll bring the snacks and blankets for us. "He went.

As soon as he went I hovered above Lily but looking at her face she wasn't surprised. She had a cold face. Her eyes have turned dark. No sparkle or fire in her eyes.

I came closer to her face.

"I know you are making me feel vulnerable and jealous but I'm not gonna get it," I whispered near her lips. Our lips were touching if she moved a bit we might kiss.

"I can fuck you right on this couch but restraining myself because he is here," I said but she didn't have anything on her face.

"Did I stop you? " She whispered near my ear.

My dick twitches. She puts her hands on my chest and whispers again.

"But I only fuck those guys who are my style, Not you little bastard." She pushed me and made me dress properly.

Chris came back with snacks and a blanket and gave it to us. He brought only one blanket. This is going to be fun.

But I'm still shocked at how she replied to me back with a dirty little tongue. They were not cold it was something else. The face she made was rare in women whom I've met.

It looks like a merciless expression which I usually have.

He started the movie and it was boring. Like really boring. But suddenly I felt a hand on my thigh. I looked at the hand and it was Lily.

She looked at me and winked. That made my heart flutter. She pressed my thigh and rubbed her hands on my thigh. The movie ended and she got up.

"I'm sleepy right now so I'm going to sleep. Good night. " And she went just like that. Leaving me.

Me and Chris talked for a long time. He brought some wine for us. But Lily didn't come out for once.

We went to sleep. I slept with Chris as they only had two rooms.

In the middle of the night, I woke up feeling thirsty. So I went to the kitchen and drank the water.

I looked at Lily's room as a thought passed my mind. I went to her room and opened the door and to my surprise, she wasn't there.

I checked the bathroom and the whole house she wasn't there.

I sat on her bed as the bed smelled like her. It wasn't strawberry or vanilla.

It was rich with notes of leather and smoke. She smelled different and that attracted me. I was waiting for her in her room.

When the room door opened revealing Lily in a different attire. She was wearing a black leather suit which hugged her body nicely.

When I strolled down I noticed something in her hand as she quickly hid it behind her.

"What are you doing in my room? " She said with a cold face.

I went closer to her as she stood there. I pulled her to me as she kept her hands on my chest.

I was going near her neck to inhale her scent but she pushed me and I stumbled back.

When did she have so much power in her? She went to the bathroom and came back after getting changed.

I was still in her room. It was 5 in the morning when she came back.

"Where were you? " I asked as she looked at me her eyes had changed to soft.

She was wearing her normal outfit. Which was colourful.

"None of your business," She said and was going to bed but I came near her and pinned her to the wall.

She looked at me her eyes warm. "Don't speak with me like that. Where were you? " She blinked and looked at me.

Her eyes changed into darkness. She came near my lips and whispered. "I was busy with people who betrayed me. "

I looked at her lips. Where were small but plumpy lips?

I leaned in and kissed her. No one moved them. Just touching them I looked at her eyes.

Which were soft and widened. I left her lips and looked at her.

" Ho-how c-can yo-o" She stuttered up.

I chuckled at her face which was red. I went out of the room and sat on the couch.

I looked at her door but she had already closed the door.

The thing which was still on my mind was where was she? Her eyes? Her different attire?

She usually wears vibrant coloured clothes. But why now? A dark black leather full body suit.

She's so unpredictable.

Something is wrong over here. Something tells me that she is not of those girls you find at every home. No, she was rare.

_____

Vote for the next part.

11. Irenic

L ily Rose

Days passed by and he never came.

It's been a week since he had pecked me on the lips. He didn't meet me Or call me. But Chris who was with me was moving out today.

That was the most bad thing for me.

My health was more blooming than before and Chris thought to move out.

"My stay with you was the most overwhelming. I mean staying up late at night, watching series and munching up are the things I did before. I was a clean guy before meeting you. " He said while packing his bags.

"You're no fun then. " He chuckled.

"Seriously rather than living in a Mansion this small little apartment is more cute. "

"That's why I love apartments more than mansions. " I said.

"It would be fun if you stayed back more". I said sulking up.

" I would love to Lily but you should have your privacy and I would visit you regularly" He said bidding me.

We exchanged our hugs and goodbyes. It was more lonely after Chris left.

It's still early and I have no zizz left. Maybe I should go for a morning walk. I wore my tracksuit and jogged out.

This is heaven. Breathing fresh morning air is the best.

"Hi." I turned around to the source of the voice. I stopped and looked at the person who stood beside me.

"I'm sorry, I don't recognize you. "

"Oh yeah, I haven't introduced myself, right? I'm Jacob. Your neighbor. " He said.

"Oh Hi. It's nice to meet you. " I said.

"It's good to see someone new here. It's a doom neighborhood so only seniors are here. "

I looked around and saw a bunch of elderly people walking around.

"But it's nice here, the people are understanding and caring towards you. "

"Anyways I gotta new partner for a morning walk. " We talked and jogged together.

He's not so bad usually your neighbours are creepy so.

Anyway, we need to get ready for another climb to rock I mean the job.

Today nothing had happened. No work pressure or anything. Is it the calm before the storm?

"Ms.Rose you've been appointed as Mr.Carter's assistant. " She said giving me an envelope. A gasp left my mouth as the words left her mouth.

"I didn't even apply for it. I mean suddenly. "

"You need to report to Mr. Carter's cabin now. " She said keeping the envelope on my desk.

"I... What do I have to say? " I asked being nervous.

"He just said you to come in his office. I don't know what you are going to say. " She said turning away.

"Can you give me any idea?" I asked. What do I say to him? " Best of luck," She said and went away.

Like that, I mean what should I say to him?

Hello sir. Nice to meet you.

That's too informal.

Sir, you called me

Too formal.

What should I do?

I mean people usually say that he is too mean and rude.

Yeah, every billionaire CEO are like that but from department manager to CEO assistant that's too early.

Anyway, I need to pull over.

Knock knock.....

"Come in " I heard from the inside.

I'm now standing outside his cabin. Feeling nervous.

I went in and greeted him.

I looked over his seat. He was looking out and I couldn't see his face. By the posture, I can say he is sexy.

"Hi, sir. I'm your new assistant. "

"Ms.Lily Rose. " He said in his dark husky voice but yet that sound felt so familiar.

"Yeah, sir. "

"You can't leave the job until my orders. You've signed the contract saying that you will stay here for 3 years. Am I right Ms. Lily?" He said.

His voice is somewhat recognizable.

"I know that. When I was appointed that time I got a paper to sign but I did ask around and no one has ever gotten that paper, why me? " I asked as curiosity filled in me.

The envelope she gave me had a paper inside saying that I couldn't leave the company for 3 years and I had to sign that.

"You're special Lily " He said.

That voice. I know that voice more than anyone, the voice that I have started to despise yet I couldn't. He turned around

"Zaeden"

I looked over his desk and found the nameplate.

Zaeden Carter.

"Don't worry baby. You're in my hands. "He stood up and walked over to me. I stood there completely speechless.

"Why are you so quiet lil cat? " Those words from his mouth are dirty but I'm still liking it.

He came closer to me moved my strand of hair back and whispered. "You thought I would go away leaving you like that. No baby."

I moved back but he pulled me more closer to him. "Don't move or I'll throw you over my desk. " He said pulling me more into him.

"You did that on purpose isn't it? " I asked if he knew about me being in his company.

"I knew from the start Lily. When you joined my company I knew you were there. " His voice softened.

"Then why did you appoint me? " I asked. "I just wanted to," He said looking into my eyes.

I came back to my senses when I felt his face close to me. I pushed him.

"We are at work Zaeden. Act like a superior. You're my boss. " I said as he moved back. He moved back and went to his seat.

This moment is too awkward for me. "Did you do your task?" He asked looking into his computer.

"No. It's still remaining. " I said being normal.

"So why are you standing here? " He said looking at me with a cold face.

I rolled my eyes at him and said. "You called me here and now you are asking me why am I here."

"Don't roll your eyes at me. " He said in a dangerous tone.

I walked out of his cabin frustrated. How can he be so dumb?

"Hey, Lily. I heard you got promoted. " Josh said.

"Yeah. It's pretty good. " I gave him a sarcastic smile.

"Yeah, I understood that. Wanna have a coffee? " He asked me.

"I need that man. " We walked to the cafeteria.

"So how was your first meet with Mr. Carter? "

"I have never seen a dumb man like him. " I said sipping my coffee.

"Dumb? "

"Don't let me get into details. " I said.

"Lily... Umm.. "

He came and stood beside me.

"Look what happened last time was a mistake. I... "

"I'm okay Josh. I'm sorry I turned you down. "

"No, don't be you're the best person I've ever met. I don't regret anything. " He said.

"You are the best guy I've ever seen. "

"You mean sexy right? " I laughed.

"You don't find me sexy".

" I do. I do "

"You're the sexiest man I've ever seen. Happy? "

"Is that a question? " I hugged him.

" This is not a lover's park where you can hug. " Ugh! This man.

Not again.

We broke the hug and looked at the Man standing before. Of course, you might have guessed.

" What are you doing here?" I asked

"I own the company, Ms. Rose"

"Josh I'll meet you later" I said to him as he nodded and left.

I looked at him and then walked away but just then he took my wrist and pulled me into my new cabin.

"What the fuck is your problem? " I asked when he pinned me.

"Language lily." My name from his mouth sounds like heaven to me.

" Leave me Zaeden, someone might see us," I said looking around. " Let them see. "

"Are you fucking crazy Zaeden? Don't act like a possessive man. You're nothing to me. "

"After we kissed and all " I turned my face.

His hands came to my chin and made me look at him.

"Look at me when I'm talking. " He said as I landed on his dark orbs. "You can't go around hugging anyone"

"Anyone? He's not anyone he's a friend and who are you bossing me around? "

"Lily don't test my patience"

"Fuck off Zaeden" I pushed him hard and he stumbled back.

He pulled me back and..........

_____

Vote for the next part.

12.ORPHIC

Z aeden Carter.

I won't mind the things that are happening to me. But it's invariably ringing in my head and fuck I can't stop nevertheless.

She's trying to ignore me.

I pulled her into the cabin and she tested my patience. I pulled her around when she tried to get out of my presence.

I pulled her up on the desk spread out her legs and stood between them. She looked at me with her doe but sharp eyes.

I love them the most.

"Never shook me off, you're walking on a thin thread, Lily. " I said and bit her neck.

She moved back giving access. I sucked on her sweet lil spot until it turned red.

I removed my lips and looked at her. Her eyes showed rage at me. I touched the hickey as she hissed.

"Next time test my patience you might be naked under me and begging me to fuck you hard. " I said but her eyes didn't change it turned more darker.

"Not even in your dreams Zaeden Carter. I'll kick you so hard and make you dickless person." She said.

Oh fuck my whole name sounds heaven to me. What the fuck you are doing to me, Lily.

"Oh yeah, there will be a day when you will beg me to do that Ms. Lily Rose. " I gave a peck on her lips and left.

I smirked thinking over and over about the cabin thing. We have a meeting now right now and she has to attend it as my assistant.

Oh, it's so much fun teasing her. I can do that all my life.

....

We were waiting for Lily to enter so we could start the meeting.

The door opened as she walked through it. She walks like she owns the place or is that how she usually walks?

Wait, she's just an assistant of mine.

Is she popular or something?

Anyways she came and sat beside me. I looked at her. She looks elegant and sexy too.

I looked at her neck but to my surprise, there was no hickey at all. She put makeup on my love bite.

WHAT THE FUCK!!!!

I looked at her and she was looking at the front. I stared at her for a good minute when she said something.

"Stop gawking at me, you will pour a hole through my face. " She said smirking.

"I can stare at you for how many minutes I would like, It's my eyes. " I said as she turned toward me.

"Then I can rip out your eyes then you can watch me as long as you want " She poked my cheek.

She was enjoying this.

I pulled her chair closer to me as she stumbled up in her seat.

Everyone was looking at the woman who was presenting the meeting. She looked at me and gave me a look 'What the fuck are you doing'.

I gave a grin to her. She looked ahead ignoring that's what I want her to do. My hand went to her thigh as she sat frozen in her place.

Thank god she was wearing a skirt. I looked at her but her face showed nothing.

But her body was frozen. My hand went to her thigh and I lightly rubbed.

My hands went upwards but suddenly her hand jerked me off.

What a fucking bitch.

She pulled her seat where it was. I looked at her in astonishment.

Suddenly everyone looked at me. I mean everyone. I looked at Lily as she mouthed 'The meeting's over'.

I smirked and looked at everyone. "Ms.Lily, what are your thoughts on this project? "

I knew she didn't pay attention to it too. She stood up and said "I think we need to enhance it a bit more. " She continued

"We need to attract people towards this project So I think you guys need to edit a bit out. The package and the software need to be changed and for the rest, I would help. " She turned towards me.

Her face held a satisfied grin as she knew my intentions.

"Let's go with Ms. Lily's opinion and I think you guys would look forward to it. " I stood up and went outside the meeting room.

How can she read my thoughts? I can't even read hers.

I was in my cabin thinking over and over about her...

What is she? Who is she? There's something about her that no one knows.

I called my investigator. "I need all the details about Lily Rose. " I hung up without any second answer.

□□□ □□□□□□□□□ □□□□□□ □□□□□□ □□□ □□□ □□□□ □□□□ □□□□ □□□ □□□□ □ □□□ □□□ □□□□□ □□ □□ □□□□□□□□□□ . □□□□ □□□ □□□'□ □□□□ □□□□ □□□ □□□ □ □□□□ □□

Lily Rose

He's the most psychotic man I have ever met. But his touch was suddenly engulfed in me.

Did I want more?

Hell no. But when he sucked my sweet spot and touch me in a very bad way but that felt ....

Maybe I wouldn't have stopped him but I knew the meeting was nearing soon.

He thinks that I'm an old shit who would roam around his tail. Fuck him then. I'm not a sweet little woman.

I can't let anyone on me. This man has an attitude toward things.

I'm the baddest bitch people would have ever imagined. They can't think when they pull the shit out of me.

No one gets through me. The things I have suffered have taught me this. The person made me this shit.

People would shut up if they heard my name.

No one can stand up to me.

Anyways I'm going to go for a long drive to get this shit out of my head.

I went to the receptionist and told her I was leaving early as I was not feeling well and gave her the file to give to him that I made earlier because he didn't pay attention to the meeting as a revision page for him.

Zaeden Carter

I was waiting for her in my cabin to return and someone knocked on my door.

Usually Lily doesn't knock on the door she usually barges in.

"Come in, " I said. I pretending to be busy.

"Sir! " This voice was surely not Lily. I looked at the person.

She was the receptionist. She came near me and handed me the file. "Sir Lily gave it to me and told me to give it to you as she is leaving early ".

" Why did she leave early? "I asked my voice thick and hoarse.

"Sir, she said she was not feeling well. " The receptionist said.

"Keep the file here."

Did she feel uncomfortable when I touched her? Am I going out of the limit?

She kept the file on my desk and left. I opened the file.

As I read the file I chuckled. She gave me a quick preview of the meeting.

She knew I was not paying attention and that's why I asked her about it. She cares for me.

She even wrote her opinion about her and in the end, she wrote something.

If you want to change something let me know.   L.R

She does knows what I'm thinking.

Lily Rose

My car was riding at a speed of 160km. I opened the windows to let the fresh air awaken me.

I opened the side deck draw of the drawer to take out the cigarette box.

I lit the cigarette and put on my favorite song which brings me to reality. Hotline remix by Billie Eilish.

My car riding through the dark forest road and the song playing as the wind blew bringing serenity.

I took a hard puff bringing the anguish and nostalgia.

When I entered into the dark world I was 17 years old. 17 doesn't haunt me.

The first was at 14 a cigarette to decline the pay of my stepmom.

A horrible animal she was. Let men insult me and throw things at me as if I'm someone's illegitimate child or even worse.

She would throw me out of the house at night just so she can party all night and she didn't care even if it was freaking snowing.

I had to stand in the backyard. I was not even allowed to go anywhere

Not even a scarf would mind her. If I got sick she would make me work even more.

The rage of me taking a knife and dragging it into her neck would satisfy me. No one knew me if I even existed in the neighbourhood.

When my dad went for his business, I and that piece of shit moved into a new neighbourhood.

But to my surprise, my dad never came back. I waited for him but he never came. She also had new men every day to entertain her.

The breeze reminds me of the endless nights I sneaked out. It was fun.

At 17 I was learning those things that a parent would never want their child to. But things made it happen.

People would start shaking if they knew my name.

A LIGHT CAN DEVOUR THE DARKNESS BUT DARKNESS CANNOT CONSUME THE LIGHT.

Vote...

13.

Z aeden Carter

I came out of the bathroom getting freshened up. I was getting ready when I got a call from the investigator.

"Hello sir " He spoke.

"Speak up what you got," I said.

"Ms Lily Rose's dad left her and her stepmom at 14 and they moved to a new neighbourhood and after that, she was never seen again. No one even knows her in the colony.

Her stepmother usually had parties but they never saw her too. She was a non-existent person in that neighbourhood. They just knew she had a young worker working at her house but they never saw her come out and or in.

But by sources she had continued drag. She was active and She was going somewhere and that's all we got." He finished his sentence.

"Where was she going?" I asked.

"Sir we can't get that. She has nothing on her. I think she's clean." He said

"Okay. If you get any information get it to me." I said and hung up.

She has nothing on her. She's clean.

She has something on her. I can sense it even from afar.

....

I came into the cabin. She didn't come to the office yet.

I sat on the chair thinking about the information he gave.

No one knew about her existence.She had a young worker in her house.

That means her stepmom didn't treat her well. But she was active and was going somewhere.

I called the investigator.

"Hey, Can you tell me that when she was active and how many active locations you can get of her?" I asked.

"Sir, till now .... She's active. Mostly she is active but at night we can't get her information." He said

"Can you get me the details of her on the 3rd of January night?" I asked.

That night she came late in a leather suit. She was not telling me where she went.

"Sir that night she was at home. She never moved out. The CCTV shows that her car was at home. She was at home all night" he said.

"I mean maybe not her car herself alone going somewhere" I asked shocked.

"No sir, the CCTV shows that she didn't move out. No one was on that road. It was empty. " He said.

"Are you sure?" I asked. I was already in shock.

"Yes sir that's what it shows" I hung up.

What's going on? She never moved out. She did. She came in front of me.

Suddenly someone barged in.

"Don't you have manners to knock on?" I said frustrated.

"As if you have ." Hearing her voice brings me to peace. I looked at her. She was looking normal.

"Why did you go early yesterday ?" I asked with a normal face.

"Aww looks like you missed me. " She said. I think she's in a good mood today.

"Lily," I said in a dark voice. She knows I'm being serious.

"I was not feeling well" she said not looking at me.

"You feeling good now," I said as she nodded her head at me.

My eyes went to her neck.

"Looks like you forgot to put makeup on my love bite." I looked at her neck. I could see the hickey.

Her hands went up to the hickey and she looked at me.

Her eyes shone as she touched her hickey. I stood up from my seat and went toward her.

She stood there and her hands folded around her chest.

"I think you love my touches, don't you?" I asked getting closer to her

"In my dreams. Don't get ahead of yourself Zaeden."

"So you dream about me," I said as she rolled her eyes.

My legs paced up and my hands wrapped around her throat and pinned her to the wall.

"DON'T ROLL YOUR EYES AT ME?" I said.

She stood there unbothered.

My hands tightened around her as her hands came up to my hand and she suddenly turned me around leaving me in shock.

She knows how to defend herself.

"So you know self-defence," I said.

"I know more than that." She said as I turned her around.

Taking her hands back and pinning her to the wall.

"Now what you say. What will you do if someone holds you like this? " I said bringing my body closer to her.

I knew she was going to use her legs as I backed up but in an instant, she caught me off guard.

She turned me around and pinned me up so that I couldn't use my weight or legs to push her off.

" Never let them know your next step." I sighed knowing I couldn't win.

She removed me from her grips but now it's my time to play with her.

I turned her picked her up and pulled into the desk. Pinning her with my hands on both sides of the table.

I leaned in as she stood there in her place gazing into my eyes. Her eyes have a spark that keeps me within her in my heart.

"Don't play with me, Lily"

"I love to play with you Zaeden "

Just as I was leaning more someone knocked on the door. Fuck them for ruining this moment.

Knock knock.

She jumped from the desk as her leg dropped on me. I hissed from the pain.

"Come in, " She said as the receptionist entered.

"Sir, the clients are in the meeting room. " She said looking down.

"Oh yeah, you can go he will come soon," She said as the receptionist left.

"Excuse me I'm the head over here not you. You cannot argue with me. " I said

"Ohh looks like now you felt it because in the morning you didn't meet the clients so I had to. I called you but you didn't pick up. Thanks to me I saved the deal."

She said waving her hair.

" And yeah I'm not coming to the meeting and take this file and please this time pay attention to it" She said.

"Why? " I asked as she gave the file to me.

"I have some work ." She said taking her coat.

"What work? "

"None of your business," She said and left.

Lily Rose

This punk is getting on my nerves. I should take out the knife and skill it into his neck.

As I gave him the file he said to check it once again.

So I opened the file and checked it.

"Can you give me your phone? " He asked me.

"Why do you need my phone? " I asked being suspicious.

"My phone died I just need to make an urgent call. " I gave him my phone as he made a call.

"No one is allowed to open the door and I mean no one even if she screams until and unless it's broken. " He said and hung up.

"Who are you gonna lock?" I asked giving him the file.

"You " I turned around but he was at the door waving at me.

I ran towards the door but he had already locked it.

I know No one's gonna come to help because he had already got it covered.

I sighed and went towards the transparent window. I love this side of his office where you can watch the whole city.

This awakens the 15-year-old Lily who used to sneak around and go to watch the stars.

I stared at the city which felt distant people just going on here and there not caring.

Whereas I don't even care to. The world is made just to scare you and only give you a couple of moments of happiness.

I don't even know where my stepmom is and I won't ask for it. But I would love to give her a painful death.

I love calm, peaceful places they bring serenity to me even if doesn't belong to me.

I know why he didn't come to meet the clients.

I don't have much time for my other purpose to execute it.

I have many secrets buried inside me that no one has ever known. Trust issues work everywhere.

———————

I stood behind the door as the receptionist told me that the meeting had ended, so he might be coming soon.

As I heard the door click open he came inside and his head searched around to find me as I slipped out behind him.

The whole day he had to work alone without me. I know he loves to tease me but sometimes he needs to understand.

I went to the receptionist and told her that I was leaving so that she could tell the gatekeeper to bring my car.

I was in the elevator thinking about Zaeden. He might be asking for me but I have already left.

I went down and saw my car standing outside. I smiled seeing my car.

I love cars they are the most beautiful thing for me.

I knocked on the window so that he could get out and give me the key.

The window slid down as my breath hitched.

Zaeden sitting in my car.

"Surprised to see me lil cat "

_____

Vote

14.GRAZE

L ily Rose

"Surprised to see me here lil cat. "

My heart ran fast to see him here. I was not even expecting him.

Fuck how can he get here so fast? Even if he takes stairs he can't get here. The building has 36 floors and I don't think he can run that fast.

"How did you get here so fast?" I asked obviously with a shocked reaction.

"By my legs baby. "

"I'm serious Zaeden," I said.

"It's a secret little cat. "

I opened the door and sat in the passenger seat. He started the car.

"BTW where are you taking me? " I asked him unsure of where he was taking me.

"You'll get to know soon," He said and sped up the car.

"Where is this place? " I asked him where in the middle of a forest and reaching here it took 2 hours for us.

"Come with me. " He gave me his hands to hold but instead I folded my hands in my chest.

"Where are we Zaeden? If you think you can kill me here you can't -" I said but got cut in between.

"I'm not going to kill you just come with me " I took his hands and started walking with him.

We walked and walked and my legs started giving up.

He turned back and looked at me."Lily if you're tired I can pick you up. " He asked being concerned.

"No, I'm okay just walk. " I said trying to breathe properly.

He suddenly pulled me close as I collided with his chest.

"It's okay. Sometimes you can ask for help too. " He said and started walking.

After some time we reached near as I heard water falling sounds somewhere.

As we went closer I saw a beautiful waterfall. My mouth is wide open as I take in the scenery.

"This isn't over yet. " He said and started pulling his shirt out as I looked around.

I've never been to a waterfall before and it's my first time but it's so beautiful.

He came and stood behind me as I felt his hot breath on my neck.

His cold hand came in intact with my skin as his hand moved toward the strap of the dress.

I turned around to see him almost naked just with his pants.

"Don't worry I won't do anything. " He said.

" What are you doing? " I asked not being sure about his intentions.

" I need you to take your clothes off but -but just with inners. " He said.

"And why would I do that? " I asked him.

"Do you have extra clothes? " He asked as I shook my head in no.

"So you can wear it back again dumbo. " He said smacking my head.

I glared at him as his hands came around. He helped me with removing the clothes as I was wearing a heel. He removed the heels.

Now I was half naked in front of him just with my inners. He held my hand and started taking me near the waterfall.

He went in as I stood there he took a breath and came to me. "The water's cold so breath properly. " He said.

I bent down as his hand came to my waist and I lightly went in.

The water was colder than my Usual water in the bath.

I breathe in and out.

I nodded my head so that we could move ahead.

"Can you swim? " He asked as I rolled my eyes.

Doesn't he know with whom he is talking?

"I'm gonna give you a really hard punishment for rolling your eyes at me. " He said.

"And you think I'm gonna let you do that. Keep dreaming Zaeden. " I said mocking him.

"Keep that aside, can you swim? " He asked again.

"Of course Zaeden I can swim and that too professionally. "

"Okay go on ahead " He said giving me space.

Does he think I can't swim? I don't like these types of men who feel women are weak and pathetic.

I breathed in and moved inside the water to swim and show off my skills to him.

I went deep into the water that he can't see me. I wanted him to come and find me.

I went and fastly swam deep and went to the end as I stood up and peeked up he wasn't there.

I think he went in to find me. A smirk plastered on my face.

"Lil cat you're so dumb. I can read you like an open book. " He was right beside me standing.

I can't understand this man at all.

He swam ahead without waiting for my response as I swam behind him. He stopped and held my hands.

We came out of the water.

The wind blew as my body shivered. He came closer to me and attached his body to me.

"Get off me Zaeden. " I said moving out of his hold.

He pulled me closer to his body and spoke.

"Take my warmth Lily I know you don't like cold. " I was shocked. How did he know about it?

He walked sticking his body with me.

What are we doing right now? I'm his assistant and he's the CEO of the company. We are kissing but that too without my permission and now we are in the dense forest walking half naked sticking our bodies together for warmth.

Is this right? Am I going the right way? It's not about the relationship we are having but I need to plan things too before creating chaos.

"Don't think too loudly baby. I can hear it here. "

His hands came to my eyes and blocked my view.

"What are you doing? Why are you covering my eyes Zaeden? " I asked.

"Don't worry just trust me I won't push you from here. " He said and walked ahead.

After walking for a few mins he said. "Just open your eyes slowly okay? " He said as he removed his hands from my head.

I slowly opened my eyes to see Zaeden standing in front of me.

He was looking at his phone and used that time to check him out. His V line looking very fine to me. His body looks freshly worked out. His shaved face and perfect jawline.

I mean he's just 27 a billionaire and looking like a Greek god already. I am 23 a secret hidden person that no one knows about.

"So in 3 ... 2...1 look over there. " He waved his hand toward the direction.

The view which was in front of me was so mesmerizing that I can't even express it. We are at the end of the dense forest and I could see the birds moving here are there and the sun setting at a perfect site.

This is such a moment that I can't even thank him for this.

"Zaeden this is so.... Mes - mesmerizing. -I can't even express it. " I looked at him to find him staring at me already.

He leaned and caressed my cheek with his thumb. He turned my body pressed his body with me and hugged me from behind.

"Stay with this moment Lily after walking and walking hard we can see this mesmerizing scene before our eyes. " He said as I leaned into his chest.

I sighed and looked at the scene. This view was settling my heart. This relaxed me the most.

"Why are you showing this to me? " I asked curious.

"I used to come here to recover myself from my parent's death. " He said.

"Who told you about this place? "

" My grandma told me about this place. After my parent's death, my grandma was the only one I had but she was sick she said that this place was hers but she told me and said that keep this place and share it with someone you can believe and trust. " He chuckled lightly.

"So why did you tell me? Do you believe me? " I asked him.

" No. Who would believe weird women like you? " He said.

As I punched his chest lightly.

"That hurts. " He said

" It should. " I lightly smile at him.

Somehow this place is convincing and melting my heart. I never felt this light and free. Even after joining the business, I couldn't bring myself for peace and joy that I longed for.

IT CANNOT BE SEEN, CANNOT BE FELT,CANNOT BE HEARD, CANNOT BE SMELT, IT LIES BEHIND STARS AND UNDER HILLS, AND EMPTY HOLES IT FILLS, IT COMES FIRST AND FOLLOWS AFTER, ENDS LIFE AND KILLS LAUGHTER.

––––––––––––

Vote for the next chapter.

15.BLEW OFF

L ily Rose

The darkness started to surround us as we stood there watching the scenery.

"It's going to be dark soon we need to leave." He said whispering in my ear.

I came out of his grip and nodded. I was moving ahead on my own not waiting for him.

I turned my head to see him coming and jumped in the water swimming ahead.

I pulled my head up when I was near the waterfall when I saw Zaeden standing near the waterfall. He has already worn his clothes.

"How did you get here so fast? " I asked him as I didn't feel him swimming with me and his hair was already dried.

"There was another way from where you can come back. I called you but you went in the water " I groaned in frustration.

I came out and started wearing my clothes as I turned around. I couldn't see Zaeden.

"Zaeden, Zaeden,Zaeden! Could you let me know if you are here? Where are you? Where are you hiding? This is not a time to joke. " I called him but he didn't answer me.

I quickly put on the clothes and started walking from where we came.

I walked for like 20 minutes and came to the spot where we kept the car. But there was no car.

I called him again but no answer. I called on his phone.

Is he lost? No, because he has come here more than once.

Did he just leave me stranded in this dark dense forest?

I was fuming with anger. I wanted to kill him brutally for leaving me here.

I opened my phone and called Ken.

"Ken, track my location and get me a car soon." I hung up the call not waiting for his answer.

Ken is my most trusted man. I trust him because he was with me on the journey for 17 years.

After waiting for like 10 minutes a car stopped in front of me.

I sat in the back as he drove out of this place. I'm so fucking angry at him. At least he can tell me that he is leaving me here and I have to come on my own.

"How did you get here Blue? Did someone kidnapped? " He asked sounding unsure.

"No, it just happened to be. Don't worry I'm safe. "

I was having fun with him, he was acting sweet and caring with me but now he showed what he could do with me.

I want to choke him to his death. He just didn't blow me off, he also broke the bit of trust that I started to build in him.

"We are here Blue. " Ken said removing me out of my thoughts.

"Thanks, Ken for your help. I'm grateful" I said and went into the house.

I threw my bag on the couch removed all my clothes and went into the bathroom.

I need a cold bath to control my anger. He will regret what he did.

Zaeden Carter

When she turned around to pick her clothes I turned around to leave. I wanted to annoy her which I love the most.

I walked and came to the spot where we kept our car. I just made her so happy a bit of fun has to be there right?

I sat in the car and drove towards my home as it took longer to reach.

I wanted to tease her but somewhere I felt guilty she might think I'm lost or something.

maybe I could have dropped her home.

I sighed heavily and drove home.

I opened my phone and checked her location which showed that she had already reached home.

So soon how can she teach home so fast?

———————

Next Day

I just came to the company and it's an hour and Lily still didn't come yet.

Is she still angry with me? I mean that was just a prank not to harm or something.

I checked her location and she was at home. Anyways she might be here or...

I called the receptionist and asked her if Lily had taken a leave or something.

"She is in her cabin, sir. " What....

"Today she came a bit late and she did give a notice that she might be late too. " I hung up the call.

I rang the bell so that she could come here.

Knock knock

"Come in," I said as she entered. Lily knocked on my door. I never expected this.

She looked at me with her dark brown eyes which were too dark. Her eyes didn't have any emotion and no shine in them.

It lost its spark.

"Get to the point Mr. Carter. " She said.

"What? " I asked nevertheless of the question

"Why did you call me here? Don't say you need a coffee" She said.

"It's my choice if I say that you need to bring a coffee" I said speaking in the same tone as her.

"Then I'm sorry Mr. Carter I can't bring your coffee because I'm your assistant, not your maid. " She said rolling her eyes.

I got up and moved toward her but she didn't back away. I stood in front of her and said.

"Don't provoke me Or I might do something bad that you can't handle lil cat. " I whisper the last word.

"I don't fucking care we are in the office keep your business aside and work on the project. You still haven't given me the report which I sent you yesterday. " She said.

"I'm the head over here don't tell me what to do and what not. " I said.

"Oh yeah, then at least keep that in mind, Mr. Carter. " She said and left.

What the fuck she just ignored it and went to work. I went toward the transparent window which is my favorite I sighed.

This girl I can't get her out of my head some what way she comes in my mind.

I opened the CCTV and looked at what was she doing.

My blood boiled she was talking with Josh. That fucker who forcefully took her into a room.

She was talking with him as if nothing happened between between them.

Is she out of her mind?

In the end, she hugged him too.

She never came to my cabin and for coffee, she sent a staff for it.

Lily is getting on my nerves. She is doing too much now.

When the clock struck 7 I got a call from the receptionist.

"Sir Lily's mam is leaving and she has kept the file too," She said.

"Did she complete all her tasks? " I asked and I know the answer.

When it's about the work Lily never comprises. Even if she has to leave early she will complete and then leave.

"Yes sir. She and Josh are leaving together." My blood boiled. I hang up.

I opened the CCTV and looked. Josh was standing at the entrance of the lady's washroom and just then Lily came out.

She had opened her hair which dropped till her mid-waist showing her beautiful curves and she had re-applied her makeup.

They are going somewhere and that too together.

Then they moved out together. I called my valet person and told him to bring the car.

I was behind their car. They both were laughing and smiling from ear to ear.

Can't she understand that a person loves her and tried to assault her but she didn't care less?

They stopped in front of a club and moved out. Lily swayed her hips.

A club and that too which I own.

I followed them in as they went towards the VIP area.

I followed and went towards the usual suite of mine.

I watched as she hugged people and took some heavy shots.

The bartender from which she ordered her drink added something. The bartender smirked when he gave her the drink.

I was watching what would happen if she drank it.

But to my whole surprise, she threw the drink in front of his face and signalled someone.

A man who was standing in the corner wearing a black bodyguard suit came and whispered in his ear and his body left his soul.

He started shivering while Lily smirked. They moved out.

Another bartender came and started making her drink without asking her.

She's acting like she fucking owns this place.

She drank and winked at the bartender as the bartender stood there showing his positive smile.

She moved to the middle where her friends were and started dancing.

I went home without wasting any second. This woman didn't come to me the whole day and gave me silent treatment and now she is dancing with people and not caring for me.

————————

Next Morning

I woke up feeling my body sore. Last night maybe I drank too much.

The coffee makes me feel alive again. I opened my phone and checked out some messages which were sent to me.

First I checked Lily's last location. She came home at 4 in the morning. AT 4.

A message popped up on my screen.

A man in his 20s was killed brutally and was left in the middle of the road. He worked at C's club.

This club was owned by me and the man who was killed was the same bartender who served Lily.

Why was he killed and what was the purpose who killed him?

The last man who I saw him walking out was the bodyguard man who stood in the corner.

Is Lily involved in this? Does she have any connection with it?

_____

Vote

16.

L ily Rose

My night was well and fun. Josh and all my colleagues were having fun.

Josh was not bad because after our last encounter was too awkward for us so we thought to start over again.

Well, yesterday night was way too fun for me to enjoy.

But the thing that triggered me the most was the bartender.

I know I look pretty and attract a man's attention just by swaying my hips that doesn't mean he has to add Viagra to my drink.

I knew his intentions so I called Ken and made him out of my sight.

———————

Next day.

I entered the office still my head hurt with the amount of alcohol I had thanks to Chris he dropped me at home and gave me an Advil.

I knocked at Zaeden's cabin and moved in without his permission and I don't care to.

His chair was turned around I could see his back. He was looking out the clear window which I love the most in his office.

I coughed a bit to grab his attention but he didn't budge.

"Zaeden.. " I called out. I don't know why but I was feeling nervous.

Lily-Rose is feeling nervous. That sounds so ridiculous.

He didn't budge but I could hear his breathing which was uneven. He was pissed.

"Where were you last night? " He asked me. His voice was dark, hoarse and thick. That sent shivers down my spine.

I stood there not able to answer. My words were stuck in my throat. My legs have turned numb just by his words.

I looked down at my hands as I heard him turning around.

I can feel his dark heavy gaze blazing in my soul.

I don't know why but all my boldness vanished in thin air. I couldn't bring myself to speak or look up.

He stood up from his chair and came closer to me. I could feel his breath which always fascinates me and makes my legs go numb.

He took a step closer to me as I started taking a step back but before taking one more step his hand came and wrapped around my waist and pulled me closer as our chest collided with each other.

He came near my lips and whispered.

"I don't repeat myself, Lily. " He said.

I looked into his eyes which were so dark I couldn't read a fucking thing.

" You're no one to ask me that Zaeden. " Finally I mustered up.

He came closer our lips brushing with each other.

"Fuck Lily don't play with me. I'm not in the mood." He said frustrated.

"What do you want me to say? " I asked.

"Lily this is important. Where were you? " He asked being more furious.

"What do you expect me to say? I was out partying with Josh. Happy? I'm gonna leave now. " I said and turned around.

He pulled me around and pinned me to the wall.

"Lily I know everything. The bartender and all. I know it's you." He asked.

I stood there knowing nothing about what was he talking about.

"What are you talking about? What bartender and all? Say it clearly " I asked.

"Yesterday you went to a party, right? " I nodded yes.

"And the bartender mixed something in your drink and you threw the juice into his face, right? " I nodded again.

"Yes, so what ?" I asked

Zaeden Carter

What is she saying? I asked her but she still doesn't tell me.

"So what? Don't act innocent didn't you kill that bartender? " I asked

"What? Are you fucking out of your mind Zaeden? Why would I kill him? " She said pushing me out.

"Lily that bartender was killed," I said but her eyes were having no emotion.

"I didn't kill him, after partying I directly came home. " She said.

"Lily, are you sure? " I asked one more time.

"I'm fucking sure about this. I don't know him too. Why would I kill him? Do I look like I could go around killing? " She pushed me back and I turned around.

"So where are you stalking me? " She asked as I turned around to look at her.

"No why would I even stalk you? " I said. I was going behind her to check if she was okay but I was not stalking.

"Oh Zaeden you were stalking, right? Speak it out I know you. " She said following me to the seat.

"No, I was not. " I can't turn around I'm having a big smile on my face.

"You're smiling. Say it. "Suddenly I pulled her on my lap as she was shocked.

"You wanna know. " I asked as her face turned red.

I couldn't stop but smile at her face.

Lily Rose

Seeing his face brought a smile to my face. He looks more cool when he smiles usually he doesn't even give a damn about it.

His hands came towards my cheek and caressed it. I felt good in his touch. It felt relief to me. All my stress and headaches were moving out.

I leaned into his touch. I looked into his eyes. His eyes shined in love and I knew this feeling.

His eyes went towards my lips as mine too. He looked into my eyes. I felt an uneven feeling in my stomach.

He moved towards my lips as I looked at his face.

Lily, you can't do this. Lily, you can't distract yourself with these things.

I know this is wrong but I can't. I agree I have many things to do and I can't distract myself this will be a major response to my lead.

Maybe I'll regret everything later but now I won't.

And I felt his lips. It felt like heaven when his lips touched mine. I held his face and kissed him. I couldn't resist.

I kissed him more passionately. He bit my lower lip and used this chance to pull his tongue inside my mouth. He pulled me more into his lap.

My hands went to his hair as I caressed it. I felt a havok inside my stomach.

He got up with me in his lap and I felt a surface under me. He put me on his desk.

The kiss turned rougher as his hands came towards my shirt and before he could unbutton it.

Someone knocked in. In an instant, I jumped out of his desk and straightened myself. He looked at me as I looked at him. I turned around as blood rushed to my face.

I went to the door as the receptionist came in and looked towards us. I went to my cabin.

This is so embarrassing. How can I face him now?

I sat in my cabin and started completing my tasks of the day.

I can't run into him. At least not today. I would sit late in my cabin.

I called the receptionist and asked her if Zaeden left or not. He has left already and no one is in the office.

"You guys again argued right? " The receptionist asked.

"No way "

"Because you guys were so awkward and your face was red so I thought you guys argued. So why was your face red? "

I was shocked. What should I tell her?

"Ohh.. Ye. Yeah. We argued. " I stutter

She might have known about it.

I came out of my cabin and went towards his cabin to keep the file of the day. He has a meeting tomorrow early morning and I need to keep the contents. So that he can remember about it.

I walked out and saw the lights of the office are shut just the passage ones are on.

I went to his cabin and kept the file on his desk. I turned around to leave but someone held my hand and turned me around.

I can smell his Cologne from here. I didn't scream but I was scared for hell.

I was on the desk and still couldn't see anything.

"Fuck Zaeden you scared the death out of me. " I said keeping my hands on my chest.

" So you recognised me lil cat " I felt thousands of butterflies in my stomach. His dark hoarse voice near my lips.

"Zaede.. " Before I could speak anything he kissed me. I kissed him back. I couldn't say anything.

This kiss meant many things to me. Even if not to him. This meant to me.

My hands moved to his hair.

He moved to my neck and started giving wet kisses on my neck.

"Za.. Zaeden. " He stopped and looked into my eyes.

" I'm going to fuck you hard so hard that you have never imagined lil cat. "

———————————

Vote for the next part.

17.

(▢▢▢▢ ▢▢▢▢ ▢▢▢ ▢▢▢▢▢▢ ▢▢▢▢▢▢▢.)

Lily Rose

I looked at him when he said those words waiting for my reaction.

He came closer to me and whispered against my lips.

" I want to fuck you hard, rough and painful enough to remove that brat attitude that you have."

My smile grew bigger as I said against his lips.

"Do it then" He didn't take a minute to crash his lips against mine.

Hard rough as he kissed my lips. We both were dragging ourselves into this shit but still, I'm gonna love it.

The more he makes me the more I'm gonna have.

He kissed down to my throat. His tongue took every inch of his mouth. My skin burnt wherever he touched me.

I moaned between the kiss as my hands buried in his soft hair.

I heard a ripping sound and when I looked down I was almost naked in front of him.

He had already removed my shirt and the pencil skirt I was wearing.

My hands unbuttoned his shirt as he kissed my neck leaving the red marks.

I hissed when he bit my fresh hickey. I moaned out when he found my sweet spot behind my ear.

I could feel the adrenaline taking over my body as he explored my curves.

His hand moved down from my neck to the thin strap of the tank top that was covering my breast from this beast.

Ripping it with ease and exposed to his hungry gaze.

It was enough for him to bring ourselves into another kiss as his hands massaged my breast, slowing circles on my nipple, playing with it but my moans were muffled by our kiss.

His touch burned my skin and felt wrong but in such a pleasurable way.

His hands came down to my core and I felt myself getting a waterfall over there.

He played with my black thong elastic lacing it up.

"Looks like you're already wet for me lil cat. " He said as he removed my thong with one swipe.

His fingers played with my clit and I was getting sexually frustrated with this man.

I know what he's trying to do with me and I would never beg for this man.

With one simple movement, Zaeden turned me around and now I was lying on my stomach on this desk.

His hands slapped my ass hard and I could the marks on his hands.

"You have such a beautiful ass, Lily. " He whispered as lips planted slow kisses on my back.

His hands once again came in contact with my ass as I felt his hard cock against me.

I heard the unbuckle of the belt and I gasped as I felt his hard cock at my entrance.

He roughly pulled my head back and I met his siren eyes which were dark and filled with lust.

"Eyes on me as I fuck you lil cat. " My body froze at his words.

"So wet for me lil cat. " He whispered.

Holding his gaze he pushed himself inside spreading my wetness, stretching me out as I cried. My moans mixed with his groans as he started moving inside me.

Fuck Lily " he groaned, moving in and out of me at a slow pace. I moaned, pushing my hips back, taking everything I could from him.

He threw his head back, closing his eyes "Damn it" he rasped, slowly pulling out of me only to push himself in again "You feel so fucking good"

Zaeden had full control over me and that was exactly what I wanted.

He let me adjust to his size with slow sloppy movements but once he heard my moans getting louder and impatient, his thrusts became more insistent and rough with his free hand on my ass gripping it with force.

His other hand roughly tugged at my hair as he thrust relentlessly into me and the sounds of his skin colliding with mine filled the room, turning me on even more.

My gaze was locked on him and the way he was pounding into me, hitting just the right spot each time, sending me into a fiery ecstasy.

I was high, so fucking high that I didn't even care if someone can see us or hear us right now, my moans becoming uncontrollable as wave after wave of pleasure were colliding in my body in sync with Zaeden's ruthless thrusts.

His hand that was wrapped in my hair roughly pressed my head down causing me to muffle my moans as he continued to pound into me, hitting the exact spot and I could hear his soft groans mixed with curses.

"Fuck, lil cat" he hissed pulling out of me completely only to slowly enter me again, making me feel every inch of his cock filling me "You are fucking heaven".

I knew I was close and his words mixed with the feeling of having him inside me was more than I could take. It was hard for me to keep my eyes open, but he was enjoying this way too much.

This seemed to stimulate him, increasing his pace to such an extent that the whole desk shook beneath us from his relentless thrusts.

It was all more than I could bear. I let out a loud cry, my whole body shaking as the orgasm took over my body, making me shake underneath him, feeling my legs soft as Zaeden continued to pound into me making it even better and more satisfying for me.

It was hard for me to catch my breath after this and I was a freaking mess on the desk, barely keeping my eyes open. Zaeden was gripping my ass so hard, his mouth partly open, his eyes focused down where our bodies collide.

"Ahh shitt" he cursed softly under his breath, making a few more quick thrusts before freezing inside me, relaxing his trembling body onto me. He groaned, his sound filling the room as I felt his warm breath on my neck.

I saw him resting his tattooed arm on the desk, clutching the table in a grip as his orgasm took control over his body. The veins on his arms stood out as he cursed again and again, his messy hair covering his sweaty face.

And as I was breathing heavily still trying to process everything that happened, feeling how sore and satisfied my pussy is thanks to Zaeden. My ass was burning, probably having his hands prints on my cheeks but it was so fucking worth it.

I closed my eyes feeling myself getting tired and I could only his last words.

"It was worth Lily. "

Zaeden Carter

This was unexpected but when I looked into her eyes which held me captive in her possession made me lose it.

I fucked her hard and rough.

She let me do it. She was screaming my name under me. Her body was screaming for me.

It was music to my ears. I had fucked so many girls but I can't get over her moans.

I brought her home. My home. This was against my rules to bring a woman in my house but I couldn't help but bring her here.

I was through my house when I met my caretaker and the most lovable woman.

Adri. She was in her forties but she is sweet and kind to everyone.

" Who's this woman Zaeden? " She asked looking into my arms where I held LilyLily.

She was peacefully sleeping in my arms like a cute kid.

"She is my secretary " I said looking at lily.

"Ohh so she is the one you were talking about. "

I looked away. I can't keep things away from her. She is like my guardian to me.

I tell her everything and she knows that I'm a psycho killer that nobody knows of.

"Go take her to the room. She looks so tired. Do you want me to bring anything for you?". She asked as I shook my head in no.

" You can go and sleep I'll take care of her. "

I brought her to my room and changed my clothes and hers.

She was wearing my white shirt and it felt so fucking beautiful on her.

I want to see her like this every day. I can't fucking have it with me.

I slept beside her keeping her close in my arms. I'm not drunk but still, I feel myself drunk in her presence.

———————————————

18.Ignorance

L ily Rose.

Sometimes we regret everything that happened in our lives.

Why was I born?, I should have died when I got the chance.

Some things are meant to hurt and kill you with that curiosity of WHY.

Well here I am in an unfamiliar room and no one beside me and it makes me feel bad.

I know he carried me to his house but he can't stay with me and coo me a little.

Does he regret having sex with me? Because he was the one that asked me.

I had a shirt around me and it smelled like him. The dark leather and smoke lingers on his shirt.

I looked beside me and there was a note kept. I read it.

I'm sorry lil cat I had to rush over to the office. You can shower and there are extra clothes for you and go downstairs you will meet Adri.

Adri that rings some bells. He did tell me he had a caretaker equal to his guardian.

I freshened up and he had kept some clothes that matched my taste and size.

Psychotic bastard.

I headed down towards the kitchen and met a woman.

She was in her forties. A beautiful caretaker and a bastard creep. How does she manage him?

"Hey Lily, I'm Adri. Zaeden must've told you about me. " She said bringing a plate full of morning delicacies.

She's comfortable with me which means she sees me as an equal person. Gosh, that surprising.

"Yes, Zaeden did tell me about you but not much. " I said licking my lips in awe as I looked down at the plates.

"Well, Zaeden did tell me a whole lot of things about you. " She said as blood rushed to my cheeks.

"I'm sorry but Zaeden had to leave early but he said he has a meeting today and can't miss it. " She said.

" Oh shit I forgot Mr. Manuel was going to come. Fuck how can I forget something like that? " I said holding my head and looking for my phone.

" It's okay don't worry. " Adri said but still Zaeden didn't pay much attention towards the meeting.

Unbelievably he's a goddamn billionaire but how did he manage to do it even if he's not interested in meetings.

I opened the phone just to see a message popped.

From Zaeden:Well don't worry lil cat I'm going to listen to all the meeting points and let you know by myself.

I smiled at his message and texted him back.

Me:You better listen or I would kill you for that.

I closed my phone and ate the delicious breakfast made by Adri. I think I love her too.

After talking and busting myself with those foods I had some work.

I needed to meet Ken and he's going to give me a big earful for that.

I said goodbye to Adri and took a cab to the office. My car is still there. I have already sent the file of today's meeting to the receptionist.

Zaeden has made it clear for me to take a day off so I had to.

I went to the parking lot to take my car so I could rush to the dungeon.

As I was nearing my car I felt someone following me.

I didn't rush, I was normally walking to my car when I felt them coming too near.

My hand fled up as that person but I used my leg instead but they caught that too.

"Well, Blue you still haven't forgotten the tricks yet. " My breath relaxed.

"Fuck Ken I was almost going to get a heart attack," I said.

"Well, you didn't come over to the meetings and I had to take care of it. " He said.

"I do have a job now and I need to focus on that too. " I said.

He pinned me to the car. His hand was around my throat and his other hand pinning my hands behind me.

"I know everything Blue. This was not meant to happen and don't tell me you did those shit to trap. " Ken said strapping my neck more.

"I was just swayed by emotions. That was never meant to happen I know too. " I said biting my lips.

"Swayed by emotions?" He asked taunting my words back at me.

"Ken you know-.. " He cut me off saying.

"Lily Rose get your shit up. You know we are already getting behind. We still have to catch them. I'll always say don't let emotions take over you. " He said his hands gripping my neck harder.

If he calls my whole name that means it gets serious.

My face turned red with the lack of oxygen until I heard a gun-clicking sound.

My gaze turned towards Ken he looked at me and nodded.

His grip loosened and I heard a familiar voice.

"Leave her you bastard Or you die right by my hands I would love to give you a slow death. "

I relaxed and looked at Ken to see him smiling. Oh gosh, that can't happen.

No no no shit.....

Zaeden Carter

After texting Lily I knew this girl might come to the office even if I gave her a day off. Instead, she sent the files of today's meeting to the receptionist and told her to give her the minutes.

Does she not believe me enough? Well, this meeting is boring if Lily came here we could make it interesting.

But something felt wrong to me. She didn't text me that she was going somewhere and Adri called me saying she had some work so she left.

She might come for her car as we drove home in my car. I called the valet and let me know if she would come.

I checked through the cameras and looked at her after the valet called that she came in. She looked beautiful even after I ruined her.

Maybe she needs more. Baby don't worry I'm here to fulfill you.

Shaking my thoughts I looked at the screen but my breath hitched. Rage scratched through my body.

A guy who looked quite familiar to me was choking Lily but she still seemed normal to me.

She was talking with him as if it was his abusive boyfriend.

I ran towards the parking lot. My rage taking over my body. How can he touch her?

My gun clicked in his direction as I reached down.

When my voice rang towards them Lily relaxed but suddenly she tensed looking at the guy.

His grip loosened and he turned around. I have seen him somewhere but I can't remember it.

Lily's hands came towards him as she gripped his arms.

My body was shivering with rage. I moved ahead and cocked my gun at his head.

He looked at me and smiled.

"Finally I met you, Mr. Carter. " He said with a sly grin.

My gaze turned towards Lily she was looking somewhere else bored with this conversation already.

I lowered my gun sensing no danger.

"Ken let's go I'm not getting into this conversation. " Lily said looking at the guy.

Ken that doesn't ring any bells but still I have seen him somewhere.

That guy backed away and sat in Lily's car.

Are they going somewhere together?

"Lily, what's happening here? " I asked my voice dark and cold.

"Well, he was not choking me he just kept his hands on my neck. " She said her eyes glistening with truth.

"Can't you fight back like usually do with me? " My anger might be visible in my eyes.

She sighed and looked behind at the guy Ken. He was looking at his phone.

"Don't tell me he is your boyf-" She cut me off before I could complete my sentence.

"No, he's not for fuck sake stop jumping into assumptions. " She said

"Well, there's nothing for you to worry about. He's my friend and he's a good person I know from the heart ." She said.

My hands grabbed her throat as I pushed her back to the car. My whole body crashed into hers.

She can feel my hard bulge on her stomach as she whimpers lightly.

"Everything about you is mine. Even if I hate it or not you should get that to me. I can bend you over this car and fuck you out of your senses. " I said the last sentence in her as her breath hitched on my words.

She looked at me as her face was red with embarrassment.

I backed away feeling rejected without her touch. I looked at the guy and then went into the office giving Lily a last glance.

This girl doesn't stay in one place. Once I get over something it crashes in again. How can I sit back normally? Her words still linger in my mind.

He's my friend and I know from the heart.

I'm really curious about her life. Her life was equal to non existent person yet she seems a normal person.

She might feel that lonely desperate desire for love and kindness but no it's nowhere in her eyes.

I'm gonna get crazy. Lily's life is a secret tunnel that no one can get over.

It's been 9 hours and she hasn't called me yet or not a text too. Her location isn't traceable anymore.

What if she's into some criminal things? Well I don't care then she's a superwoman to me.

Ting.....

I open my phone in a hurry to see that her location is traceable.

I get my keys and drive to the location of her.

I'm gonna need her to fuck tell me about her or I'm gonna get crazy.

It's near her house but now she is turning and going towards other route.

It's until she stops at Chris House. She didn't answer any of my calls and texts and thought to give a visit to who? .

Chris.

I saw Lily getting out of the car and running towards Chris and hugs him desperately.

My blood boils with this image. I go closer and cough between them so they could hear.

Chris comes and hugs me while Lily's shocked to see me.

□□□'□ □□□□□ □□□ □ □□□□ □□□□□□□□□□ □□□ □□□□□□□□ □□ □□□ □□□□□ □□□.

――――――――

VOTE AND COMMENT..

19.Illicit

Lily Rose

I know today is just not my day. I had so much pending work left at the dungeon and it is still irritating me.

In the morning I had a little fight with him but it ended in his way and I hadn't seen Chris in so much time.

So I came to meet him. Mr. Raphael and Mrs. Raphael wanted to meet me for so long and she always thinks of me as her daughter and welcomes me as her own.

I haven't felt in years the motherly love and tender effect of her love that can never expressed in words.

I started loving her presence and I knew this wouldn't be for too long before I disappeared from their life.

What would they think of me? Did Lily care about us Or she just used us? Did we mean anything to her?

I can't even think if that happens. My heart has closed down too long ago and I won't be able to open it.

My life is full of mystery and I know Zaeden wants to know everything about me. My every truth is known by Ken.

He is my saviour but still doesn't count. I have been through so much that no one can tell what has happened to me.

I know I live like a normal person so people don't catch up on me.

Cough cough.

I broke my presence from Chris's arms to look around at the voice.

Zaeden.

The fuck. What is he doing here? I open my phone to check and now I know....

He caught my location with him. I know he tracks my location with him.

"Hey man how are you? Long time no see huh? " Chris asks as Zaeden's gaze crashes mine.

He has a dark grin on his face. Oh no something's gonna happen today.

"Nothing just been busy with work and.. " He looks at me. "I just came to meet mom have been missing her for so long. " He says.

"Well, she would be crazy to hear that you're here to meet her. " Chris turns around and looks at me.

"Come let's go inside it's freezing out. " Chris says as his hands come around my waist and pull me towards him.

"What the fuck Chris do you want me to die? " I ask. I have told Chris all about us except the night at his house. He might disappointed.

"Let's see what happens?" He whispers and turns around to look at Zaeden.

"Come in Zaeden. " I look at him his jaw clenched hard and he comes around me to stand beside me. God, I hope you help me with this shit.

Chris walks down the hallway still his hands on my lower back and I know he is doing this to make him angry.

I hope he doesn't kill me with that rage.

"Oh my gosh, Lily and Zaeden. Welcome home." Chris's mom comes and hugs both of us. I felt relieved with her touch.

I and Chris's mom sat on the couch as Mr. Raphael, Chris and Zaeden were on the patio.

I could feel the raging gaze on my back. I know he's looking at me from time to time. Chris's mom talked with me about Chris's childhood and all.

"Mom, How much are you gonna talk with her? She's tired." Chris says as he comes towards us and sits beside me.

"I'm gonna go in the kitchen. So you guys can talk and she was not bored at all. "Chris's mom says as she leaves.

I'm sure he's gonna kill me.

His hands inappropriately come around my waist. I look at him in confusion.

"Chris don't. " I say as his hands start moving making me tickle. I start laughing hard.

"Chris D.. Stop... D. Don't" I laugh as his hands lose their grip.

I hold his hands and put them behind his back as I move closer to him.

"Don't try me Chris it's gonna be bad for you. " I whisper in his ear. Chris smirks and comes closer to my ear.

"You know what Lily, Zaeden has been watching us with glary eyes. Well, I can be saved but your legs might... " He says as I hit his chest playfully and walk towards the kitchen.

"Oh Lily why are you here? Go and sit. I'll bring all the food. "Chris's mom says as she helps the servants.

"It's okay Mom I want to help. " I say as I move towards her.

"Okay well you won't listen so bring this I'm going to the dining room. " She says as she goes away.

I gathered the plates and dishes as I felt someone's presence behind me.

Before I turn around to see who it is I'm pinned to the counter. I feel his hot breath on my neck as he moves my hair to one side.

"Are you trying to push my limits lil cat? " I bit my lip hard as he kissed my neck.

"Are you trying to make me jealous? Because I'm getting jealous and I want to kill Chris. " I gasp as he moves his body closer.

I can feel his hard bulge rubbing to my back. I hold his hands to stop him.

"Stop Zaeden... Someone might see us. " I say stuttering.

"Do you think I care? Well, you didn't stop Chris too. " He says planting wet kisses on my neck.

"Lily, do you need my help? "Chris's mom asks from the dining room.

"A.. N.. No, I'm coming." I say as I push Zaeden.

"You are a shameless man. " I say and leave to the dining room. I'm a bit angry to be exact sexually frustrated.

I went to the dining room to help Chris's mom and sat beside Chris.

"Where were you ?" Chris asks me whispering. "I was just figuring to bring what? " I lie of course I can't tell him that I was with Zaeden.

He is going to tease him more and more until he breaks out and fucks me on this table.

I was still talking with Chris when I heard footsteps nearing us.

I turn and look to see Zaeden standing and looking at me with devil's eyes.

I'm fucked up. God, please help me.

Zaeden comes and sits beside me. We started eating and everyone was busy on their own.

Me and Chris were talking as Zaeden talked with Mr. Raphael and Chris's mom.

I felt a hand on my thigh as I looked down just to find his hands. He showed no emotion on his face so I let him keep his hands on me.

Until I felt him rubbing my thigh vigorously. I looked at him but still, he was having his conversation as if nothing happening down the table.

I'm not getting a good feeling about this. I pushed his hands off me and talked with Chris.

I felt him gripping my thighs hard as his hands moved towards my inner thigh.

"Zaeden the fuck are you doing? " I ask him whispering feeling obnoxious rage in me.

"Nothing just playing with my girl. " He pushes the word my girl on me.

"Do you want me to show you the pictures that Lily took of us? " Chris asks.

This guy is gonna make me die today.

"Us? " Zaeden whispers in my ear as he pushes my underwear to the side.

I look at him as I hold his hands desperate to stop.

Chris takes my purse unlocks my phone and opens the gallery.

"Ohh she even had made a separate album for our pictures. " He shows me the phone and looks at me with a sly grin.

"Don't," I beg him as he winks at me.

"Look Mom don't we look cute together? " Chris says showing my phone to his mother.

"Together? " Zaeden says mocking him as he pushes a finger inside me without letting me adjust.

"Zaeden stop... They might see us. " I say whispering to him. Must say I was pleading with him. I bite my lip hard to stop those noises wanting to scream loud.

"Let them know that I'm fingering my girl. " He says.

"Where did you guys go? "Chris's mom asks.

Don't say it, Chris.

"To date. " He says.

"Date? " Zaeden repeats his word.

"Yeah." He says

Two fingers in...

I bite my lip hard to stop the gasp and moans from my mouth. It's making me more turned on by the fact of getting caught but with Chris's mom. No.

"Date lil cat. Well, you never went with me. " He says mocking me. Whispering into my ear but I can't hear it because I'm too busy with the fingers inside me.

I'm too busy to hear the shits he has to say. I'm focused on the fingers that our working inside me. Bringing me to the world of ecstasy.

"Oh my gosh, are you guys kissing? "Chris's mom says with widened eyes.

I look at him with wide eyes. He shakes his head knowing nothing. We never kissed each other.

Two more fingers go in. Oh fuck I can't really can't.

"Did you kiss him, Lily-Rose? " Zaeden whispers in my ear with pure rage. I shake my head as words cannot be formed right now.

I'm gonna kill him if he says more than this.

"Then what's this? " She shows us the picture which is dark and you can't see properly.

It looks like we are kissing but I was grabbing a chips packet from down as our face creeps close.

"No Mom we are not Kissing it's just that when I was sleeping with her this scene happened. She was just grabbing the packet and I just crept close to her. " He says breathing out.

Zaeden moves his hand faster than ever to keep my moans muffled.

"Zaeden.. " I beg as my hands prick his legs hard.

I want to scream hard he is pinching my folds and it turns me more than on.

He suddenly pulls out of me as I moan out. LOUD.

"What happened? " Everyone asks concerns showing on their face except Zaeden. I look at him as he grins slowly.

"Umm. ye.. No.. I'm just tired Mom. I'm having a headache. Today so been a hectic day. I just want to sleep. I'll just head home. " I say

"Okay, I'll drop you. " Chris says as he gets up.

"I'll drop her. "

_____

20.Illicit 2

L ily Rose

"I'll drop her".

Do I look like a Fucking doll or something that they need to drop me? I'm not a fucking teenager who needs someone to drop.

" I can go alone too. " Everyone looks at me and I just can't avoid the raging gaze beside me.

"Lily you're tired, you can't go alone let Zaeden drop you off anyway he's going home too or you can spend the night here. " My eyes widened at her response.

If I stay here I might get saved from this devil and there's no way he would get me home SAFE.

Suddenly I feel Zaeden hands on my thighs squeezing it hard.

Our gaze mixed. Actions are speaking louder in his eyes. He wants me to go home with him. But I am scared of the fact over here.

"I.. I'll spend the night," I said stuttering up. Zaeden gets up in a rage and leaves the room.

"What happened to him?" Mr. Raphael asks.

"Maybe he got a call or something," Chris says.

_____

After the dinner or you can say after Zaeden left the table and after that, I didn't see him.

Chris made me comfortable in the guest room and helped with the clothes as it was busy and cold out there.

"Did Zaeden left?" I asked with a curious tone.

"No, he's staying in here tonight," Chris said taking the water jug.

"Where will he be staying ?"

"He has his room here." I furrowed my brows in confusion.

"I mean we have been a family from middle school and Zaeden is more like my big brother to me," Chris says

"Sleep tight Princess," Chris says as he leaves the room.

Something's wrong here. I feel a bad vibe.

Suddenly I feel thirsty and that fucking bastard took my water with him.

I open the door and look around the corridor to see if anyone is there.

Without making much noise I walk downstairs while tip-toeing.

I open the refrigerator and take out a chilled bottle.

I gulp down the water feeling my body relaxed and fresh. I keep the bottle in and move around

I just to find Zaeden's standings there. He leaned on the door with folded arms, sleeves up.

I can see his tattoos and veins popping out.

He walked closer to me as I moved back. Fucking shit this is. Why do I feel my body getting turned on? He walks closer till I feel the counter behind me.

He pushes me backwards and opens my thighs to stand between them. I feel blood rushing down and aching my arousal.

He touches my thigh lightly as I stretch my back.

"Didn't you have enough fun with Chris today didn't you Lil Cat?" Zaeden whispered as fear rushed down my spine.

Before I could say anything his hands were more fast as he plopped me down on his shoulders.

"What the fuck are you doing Zaeden? If anyone sees us we are dead." I say kicking my legs.

I feel a hot burning sensation on my butt. He just fucking smacked me.

"As I said I fucking don't care. The moment you walked into my office you were mine. Fucking get it ." He walks to his car as if he was ready to take me.

He backs me into the seat comes around and sits.

I was in the driver's seat.

"What are you trying to do?" I ask unsure of his intentions.

"Drive to this location," he says as he gets comfortable in his seat.

I rush down the engine to this location. I don't drive like a beginner, I'm more like a race driver. I open the window to my side to breathe out.

It's been a hectic day and now we are going to a strange place. It's gonna take a 30 mins to reach us.

"Do you have a cigarette?" I ask Zaeden as I get relaxed in my seat.

I feel his hands on my thighs as he yanks and plays with my night shorts.

He opens his wallet and takes out a cigarette.

"You smoke?" He asks.

"Hmm," I light up the cigarette and take a puff.

I close my eyes feeling the fresh air and the toxic nicotine take over my body.

"Do you wanna talk ?" I look over to him

"You brought me to talk ?" I ask skipping the question.

I rush the engine as we get closer to the location and my heart gets climbed up. I looked at Zaeden as he was already looking at me.

His sly smirk on his face tells me that this is going somewhere else.

"Where are we going? " I ask.

I stop the car and look at Zaeden as he gets out and walks to my side.

He leans down to my ear and says.

"In the forest where no one can hear you. "

He opened the door and put me into the back seat.

"Za.. Zaeden what a-are you doing?" I ask

"Is my little cat getting scared?" He says as he opens the door and hovers above me.

His hands go around my face as grazes my lips with his thumb.

"Did you kiss Him, Lily?" He asks me as I roll my eyes.

"Does it matter?" I say in a frustrated tone.

His fingers find my chin and then he's tugging my face in his direction as he looks into my eyes and says.

"It matters. It matters to me, Lily." He says as his hands run through his hair which I have been dying to touch.

I kiss him. For the fucking touch of my life. I kiss him badly not for lust or desire to tell him the answers through my actions.

His hands come around my waist as he kisses me back.

His hands move up to cup my wrist as I hear a clicking sound.

I move back to see his face gleaming with happiness.

I move my hands upward but can't. I'm handcuffed.

"Hell Zaeden? Remove these." I snap.

"You should have watched when you thought of ignoring me," he says removing my shorts.

"I never in.. ah" he punches my nipple.

"Don't lie to me Lil cat" he says.

He unbuttons his shirt as I watch his every move and his eyes never leave mine watching my movements.

He moves his face closer to me as my breath hits. My lungs are not working anymore.

"Do I need anything to make you understand that your body works to mine? Every inch of your body is Mine. " He says as he kisses every part of my body.

I arch my body as he plops wet kisses all over my body.

"Zaed.. Zaeden removes the. These cuffs. " I say words not standing with my voice.

"This is your punishment lil cat bear it. " He says as he tores my shirt open.

I try yanking my hands but it's impossible because the door and my wrist are cuffed.

I'm already naked in front of him but do I feel ashamed right now?

Of course not.

I feel him kissing me with all the rage he kept through all day.

He comes down to my neck as he bites leaving the red marks.

I feel his hands on my breast as he plays with my nipples.

I arch my back feeling the ecstasy taking over my body. Overflowing the pleasure as I still try yanking my wrist.

I feel his shaft on my entrance as I moan out his name.

He pushes his shaft Inside me without a warning. Tears rush down my face.

He starts moving without giving me time to adjust myself. His pace was getting faster every second. I need to hold him, hold him closer to me.

I moaned hard as I felt his hands playing with my clit while he fucked.

"Does this make you feel good lil cat? " I nod.

More tears roll down my face as he fucks me hard in his car in a forest of nowhere.

"Didn't You"

Thrust.

"Understand when"

Thrust

"I tell you "

Thrust

"That. "

Thrust

"You"

Thrust

"Are"

Thrust

"Fucking."

Thrust

"Mine"

I screamed hard as an orgasm rippled through my body.

He removes the cuffs and starts kissing harder as my hands move towards his neck pulling him closer.

"Fucking shit Lily what are you trying to do with me? " He mumbles between the kiss.

I scream hard when I feel him moving inside me. My legs are numb and my whole body is sore with all his bites.

————

After fucking for like what felt more than 2 hours. When I felt my eyes closing on their dreamland I heard his voice.

"I love you, Lily. "

21.

Z aeden Carter

"I love you. "

I'm fucking crazy I know too, I mean was that crazy when I said her my feelings after getting jealous and then fucking her hard.

That was crazy of you.

My being jealous is ridiculous but I can't let myself just look when he is touching her, laughing and then whispering to her that makes her cheeks red.

My blood boils that he is making her blush, not me. It's not jealousy in my words it's a possession that I hold on her.

Would it make any difference if I said I was more than in love with her? I'm not just looking for some quick fuck or something. A lifetime beat that makes me feel heaven with her even if I'm not allowed for that.

I'm feeling emotions that I never felt or that I was not allowed to. Being a killer makes a person not feel any kind of emotion that gives the person a need to think that they can be saved.

Anyway, I'm going overboard.

I confessed to her and guess what?

she smiled fucking smiled and then slept. She had a hard day and then I went crazy on her.

I brought her home cleaned her and then made her sleep. I texted that bastard Chris that she's staying at my house.

I walked towards the room and my heart beat fastened as it never did.

I saw her, her face beaming with the moonlight shining in.

Her plumy sore lips were ruined by me. Her sore body was covered with thin sheets and her little snores seeped in.

I smile. Her face brings calm to my body. I walk closer and slowly go on to the bed sleeping beside her as I pull her closer to my body.

Her hands come around my torso pulling me more closer to her body.

"Good night lil cat. "

––––––––––––

I look at the woman sleeping beside me peacefully. Her face makes me feel alive. Her black hair covered her face as I slowly without making her awake put behind her ear.

Wait am I drooling over her? Of course.

I lightly take her hands out of my body that hugged me last night as I walk downstairs to make her breakfast.

After making some lightweight breakfast for her I walk towards the room with coffee in my hand.

As I open the door I feel a pillow thrashing my face. As I look up my eyes widen when I see Lily dressed in my shirt. Just a shirt on her body.

I look up at her eyes as her eyes are red. The anger is flaring in the air. I keep the coffee on the desk.

"What happened? " I ask my brows furrowed

She comes forward grabs my collar and yanks me forward until her lips brush with mine.

"Never leave me alone in bed. " I look at her with my brows furrowed.

She yanks me back and walks downstairs.

Is she angry that I left her alone?

Did she have a nightmare or something?

Does she hate the thing that I wasn't with her when she woke up?

I walk downstairs and I see her making a coffee for her. I move behind her as my hands wrap around her little waist.

"I'm sorry Lily. I just went to make breakfast for you that's it. " I say with a guilty tone.

"No Zaeden last time too you left me alone and I hate that. " She says.

I push my head onto her neck feeling her dark vanilla scent.

"I'm sorry Lily that won't happen again. " I say pulling her closer.

She turns and looks at me and says.

"Promise? "

"Promise." I chuckle at her.

She hugs me as her hand comes to my chest and my heartbeat fastens.

"Is something wrong Lily? You wanna talk?" I ask why she's been acting like that.

"I just have a dreadful past that no one can ever imagine. " She looks at me with her thick lashes.

"Everything's fucked up in my life." I know she's trying not to find any sympathy or pity.

"Well that doesn't matter much wouldn't it because I'm with you. " I say my lips brushing hers.

"Well, you know what? " She says pushing me back. "It was hard to walk downstairs my legs are fucking numb. "

I chuckle at her. " Well, that means I did a good job. " I say moving closer as she takes a step back. She hits the counter as I walk closer until I'm in front of her.

I brush my lips on her neck as I hear a light whimper. I suck on the sweet spot behind her ear.

I move back and say. " We have a meeting today Ms. Rose. " I say and walk upstairs.

———————

Lily Rose

What a fucking bastard he is. Leaving me sexually frustrated is not on good terms. I walk upstairs and get ready for the damn meeting.

I was standing in front of the mirror putting some accessories on my clothes to match them. I feel someone behind me.

I look up from the mirror to see the man that I'm getting my legs and heart numb.

Water dripped from his hair. His towel hanging around his waist and I can see his v-line perfectly. The water dripping from his wet hair is making me wet.

I look into his eyes which are already looking at me. My eyes move to his lips which are plumpy and pink and I want to kiss him so bad. I see a smirk planting on his lips.

I look at him as his eyes have turned dark in black. I just have to control my legs from rubbing each other.

He comes closer and leans down to my ear and looks at me from the mirror. "It's okay lil cat you can look at me how much you want. I'm ALL YOURS. " He whispers in my ear.

I close my eyes his words vibrating my mind. Last night I did hear him confessing to me. But I don't know what love is. How to feel about them? I never felt them.

How should I confess back to him?

Do I love him?

I feel coldness when I feel him moving back from my body. I open my eyes and look at him only to see him smirking at me.

I quickly turn around and walk towards him. I walk till our chest collides and our faces in mere inches apart. He looks down at my eyes until I see his smirk fade.

I get on my tip toes to match his height and lean to his ear. My hands on his shoulder to lean down more as I bite his earlobe.

"I know how much of I own you as much as that you too. I know when you just stare at me in the morning. " I wink at him as I move back and go downstairs.

If he wants to play this game I'm on.

After waiting for like 15 minutes Zaeden comes down looking hot as always in his suit. Their sleeves rolled up, their first two buttons open and his hair nicely done.

Looks like I'm drowning in the ocean or more than that. He smiles at me as I stand up from the couch. He walks closer until he is in front of me.

His hands come behind my back as yanks me closer to his body. " Are you ready Ms.Rose? " He asks.

I nod as we walk out of his house and get into the car. I smile when I look at so many messages from Chris.

Wait I didn't inform. Oh my gosh, Chris's mom must be worried.

I opened the chats and read them

: did you have fun?

: where are you, Lily?

: I'm getting bored.

: let's have some drink babes.

: wait Zaeden's not home and you too. Are you guys having fun? Leaving me?

I smile at his chats.

: okay fine I'll pray to God that Zaeden doesn't make you sit in a wheel-chair.

: Lil cat are you having fun?

: I just got a text from him that you're staying at his house. Looks like you're fucked.

: Oh shut up Chris

: were you drunk or something?

: anyways I'm okay and I can walk too. It's your fault if you haven't acted like a bitch.

"Whom are you texting? " I look at him as his eyes are on the road his knuckles have turned white. It's my time.

"No one. " I say looking out of the window. "You were blushing. " He says. "Oh was I? " I tease him.

I poke my cheek not to laugh right now. I gasp when I feel his hands on my thighs. "Did you forget your yesterday's punishment or want me to remind you lil cat?"

He looks at me with darkened eyes. I shook my head and looked out. I can't play with this guy. He's cheating with me.

"I'm not cheating it's just my way of showing you that I own you. "

_____

22. Vulnerable

Lily Rose

I'm more than glad that we have reached the office and I don't even glance back at him because our little encounter in the car can even make him aggressive.

I run inside the company at least to avoid him for now I know that I can never run away from him. I wish everyone well and move towards my cabin.

I sigh looking at all the files lying at my table. Fuck this is gonna take a long time. I sigh one more time before sitting in my seat.

I stretch my limbs from all these shit files. My hands are paining like some needle pinched In them. I look down and see the red call button blinking bright.

Zaeden has called me... I wonder what he needs this time and if he says that he needs some coffee or something I'm gonna murder him right there.

I stand outside his cabin and breath once to see what's waiting for me.

Before I could knock I was pulled inside the cabin, pinned to the wall, hands pinned up, someone's mouth down my throat. I wriggle but stop.

The strong masculine scent fills my nostrils heavily. I relax in his presence. This kiss is a craving that I want to live for always.

Waking up like this to a life of serenity but can't happen always, isn't it? He leaves my hand and attached our forehead.

I look into his deep eyes only to see my reflection. I smile with all my heart and graze his skin with my rough hands.

"Did you need anything? " I ask as I realized he had called me.

"Yes. " He breathes and says. " Because of you. I needed you. " My heart skips a beat.

I want to smile but I can't because this is not what was meant to happen. Ken always warned me about this. This should have never happened in the first place.

I look at his eyes and then push him lightly to stand properly.

"Zaeden we are in the office, we can't get people to know about us. " I say looking away from him.

US? What are we? Arc we even in a relationship? What are we even doing? Playing around?

"I don't care about them. " He says coming forward closing our distance. I move away from him.

" Just like you don't care about me too. This is fun for you, right? All we have been doing is nothing but just fun, isn't it? Maybe I heard your confession on the night would be a misunderstanding of mine right? "

I ran away from there not glancing back at his office for once. His eyes, his heavenly masculine scent and my reflection in his eyes are making me crazy.

Because I know if I look at him once again I can't never turn back.

I'm in love. I'm in love with Zaeden

I don't know what love is and what love feels like. But this is what love feels like. But I can't because I have to pay a hefty price might be someone's life too.

I call Ken and tell him to pick me up immediately. I go down but I'm stopped by the receptionist.

"Ms. Rose you have to go back to Mr. Zaeden's cabin back. He has called you urgently. " I'm taken aback by her words.

"I'm sorry tell him that I have to go back urgently. " I say and walk towards the exit. If I run away from him I won't be able to see him again.

I see Ken waiting for me in his car lighting his cigarette up. I walked towards him but I froze. "Lily!" I don't turn around. I see Ken walking toward me in rage.

I run towards his car and sit inside. I hear him calling me continuously more like his begging me. Ken comes and drives.

I see to the rearview mirror just to tear my heart. Zaeden standing there with tears in his eyes.

What have I done? I can't go back to him like this. If he gets to know why I came to him he would hate me.

I take my phone and throw it out of the window. Ken is smiling at me. " This is why I've always said not to be in their personal space. "

----

3 weeks later

It's been 3 weeks and I've not heard a single thing about him. I called the office but couldn't get his attention. He has not been coming to the office.

"Hey, Chris. "

"Hey, how are you? "

"Well, I'm fine. "

"How's Zaeden? "

"I wanted to ask you about that. I don't know few days back he came home drunken more like bathed in liquor and now he's more like disappeared. He isn't picking up my calls and is nowhere to be seen. "

I hang up. I called his phone.

"Hello, Zaeden? Are you there? " I ask being paranoid.

"Oh hey, Lily I was waiting for your call. Want to see your boyfriend? " I'm froze. My head is dizzy. The thing I feared for most was him.

"Sam.. " I say stuttering up. " Don't call me that. You have lost that identity to call me that. " He says.

Sam is my only comfortable person. My brother had taken care of me more like my own mom. But the day our mom died he hated me more like he hated my presence.

He thought I was the one who had broken this family. He thought that's why another person was needed in our life to step. He left me all alone in that bitch case.

"Why do you have Zaeden's phone, Sam? " I ask being worried. " Aww are you worried about your little boyfriend? Don't worry he's here with me. "

" What do you want Sam? " I ask not making my voice look cracked but inside I'm crushed. "Nothing I'm just doing a favour to your boyfriend and telling him about you and your plans"

No. That can't happen.

"Sam don't do it. For fuck sake leave my life. What have I ever done to you? " I say groaning loudly. " You broke my life Lily my only way to success. Look at you you have left everything behind and become the goddamn money maker you are. "

"Look there's no issue. We can talk about this to Sam. Leave Zaeden, he's no fault. " I say. " Oh yeah, I heard that he killed your stepmum. Aren't you going to take your revenge just like you did with me? "

Before I could say anything he cut the call. Oh, my fucking gosh. This was not meant to be over like this.

"Ken I need details every fucking detail on Sam. track him down Now. "

I walk towards my car. " He's in the Italian dungeon basement and I'm sending backups for you too. " I hang up not answering him. I call Rhyan the secret secretary of his mafia business.

"Rhyan I know where Zaeden tracks this phone and come with me fast we don't have time. " I hang up and drive fast.

After all the planning and everything we are standing outside the dungeon. " Rhyan they are not aware of anything. Zaeden is in the corner of the basement and I will bring him out. Lure the people out and I need Sam alive at any cost. "

"But how do you know about us? Who are you? " Rhyan asks me. I smirk and look at him. " Blue. Blue Knight. "

His eyes wide, mouth open shocked to see me here for saving their boss.

The dangerous woman of the world. No one dares to speak against me. Everyone knows how cruel I can be. No one has ever seen me. I'm always changed in presence. Rhyan won't be able to figure me out too.

The person who finds and kills every sex trafficking group in the world and yet no one has survived. All the men in this world would bow down to me if I came out revealing myself.

".- I'm sorry ma'am. " He bowed his head. "Do as I say. There should be no mistake. " I need everything carried out by plan and you know the mistake goes by a punishment right? " I say walking towards our team.

"So I want everyone to be indeed attentive through this and if injured come out through the exit we have made. " I say coldly but inside I'm nervous.

"Everyone's ready we need to start our operation. "

I hope I help save Zaeden and get to tell him everything.

_____

23.

L ily Rose

Ken is preparing a life suit for me. I don't even want to listen to his tantrums saying that I don't care and blah blah.

Ken has always been with the journey of my life. Ken always supported and believed when people didn't. The Blue Knight name was given by him.

He loved the name Blue because it suited me. And he loves me too but I always ignored his feelings. He has made a big presence in my life that I would never forget, he saved my life from hell and did save me from this nothing of a world.

He gave me a new life and is going to protect me over anything. Saved me from my psychotic family and made me the person that I am today.

Without his help I would be nowhere, no place defines for me on this earth. My life has been just about running away from it.

Yet now I have found peace in someone that brings me to heaven. Never Ken made me feel that but he did. He has touched me in a way that I can never forget about.

He has deeply engraved in my soul that I won't be able to move on from, he has taken a part of me with him. Zaeden Carter is a sin that I'm doing.

Yet I'm happily ready to be with that sin. That is the sin that completes me. I want to save him and spend the rest of my life with him. I want my soul to be deeply engraved in him.

"Lily! Where's your mind? Be focused, I don't want to lose you because of your reckless mind. " I smile at his cute tantrums.

"Don't smile you know that I hate them. " I laugh at his words. " So funny. You hate my smile, that is ridiculous. You would die to see me laughing. " I say as he smiles lightly helping me wear the jacket.

After helping me wear my jacket everyone is ready to get inside the abandoned mansion where Zaeden is abducted.

"Be safe and come back fast so that I can slap your ass for saving him. " He says. I give him a small smile as pecks my forehead.

"I will. " I nod and go off to stand with the plan carried out.

Zaeden Carter

She left me. She left me alone.And yet I don't seem to hate her, feeling abandoned again in this world of nothing. I wanted to be beside her and she beside me.

Looking around the world to see nothing but us together. Connected, joined, intertwined together to make a beautiful world.

"Ugh. What a fucking-" A hard slap comes around my face. The stinging pain leaves a mark. I look up to see Sam Arnolds.

The brother of Lily Ros- sorry Lily Arnolds. A grin lands on my lips.

What did I know about her? Her name? That's a lie. Her past? Nope. Her future? Maybe.

"You like my sister, don't you?. " He looks at me and says. I don't say anything and there's no need to.

"Well, you don't know anything about her. Why did she come into your life? Coincidence?" He laughs loudly in an utterly bad way.

"Looks like she fooled you too." He says still a laugh on his lips. "Fooled me?" I ask unsure about his intentions or talks.

"Oh, you don't know about it, do you? Blue knight. The person who holds the power within. Where everybody wants to kill that person and let that person create havoc in people's lives who don't care to take of others. "

Blue knight. The man who is creating a storm out there and yet nobody knows who's that person is. Killing every person in his sight. Nobody knows where he is or who he is. He has killed thousands of sex trafficking groups.

"Oh, my little brother you are fooled damn fooled. My sister aka your fake lover Lily Rose is Blue Knight."

My heart stings a pain lunging over my body. Lily.. Is.. Blue. "you're lying. I don't fucking believe you. " I say spitting on his face.

Anger is rushing inside me. The rage, pain, desperation and anguish are getting into my body.

" What do you even know about her? Else from her fake name and abusive stepmother? You were fooled, Mr. Zaeden Carter. She used you so that she could get deeper into her plan. "

Fooled me. Used me. Liar. Love. Fake. Sex. Cuddles. Good night sleep.

It was all a lie. Every fucking thing that happened is a lie. Whatever between us was a lie, all lies. And I got into her trap too. Such a nice actor she is.

I'm such a fool to let some fucking girl get over me easily. After everything that had happened in my life still here, I was heartbroken over a girl who didn't even love me.

"Looks like you need to put pieces into a puzzle so you might understand this game. Mr Vena Arnolds is still alive and he wants to kill his daughter Lily but she's been so good at hiding that no one can track her and her little shit."

" She took all of his hard work in just a matter of seconds which was going to be mine. She has exposed our father and he lies. And look at you it didn't take a second to to break you up. She's been running from her family and hiding at a good place."

"The stepmother she says is not true. That woman has Amnesia and she lets Lily in because she thinks it's her dead daughter. And made her like a slave. Lily still had Ken. Ken has always loved Lily in every possible way and you know what they even have had sex together."

"Ken always stayed beside her in matters of worse or good. He was a backup plan of hers. He knew every bit of her that you don't even have an idea of. She is a broken, useless and damaged woman and you loved her like she was the only person remaining in the whole universe and look what she gave you in return." He continued as his words make way towards my mind.

His words are blurring in my ears. Everything he said is replaying in my mind. Vena Arnolds the father of Sam and Lily Arnolds is alive. Lily was hiding behind my back so she could do her work and get into my mafia.

She racked inside my skin and I let her do it. My heart never beat for anyone yet It did beat for her. Her eyes shone, her smile, her laugh everything was fake.

My body is not ready to listen to this. Ken always liked Lily? I knew something was wrong with him. The way he would look at Lily and they even had or are having a relationship.

I don't know and I don't want to but my heart is stinging with pain. The moments we shared were so beautiful yet a mess. I believed when she had opened up to me just to know that it was a lie too.

I have never given a chance to anyone not even Chris or his family to see through me but I did let Lily. I let her because she was the first woman to not look back at me. She didn't even dare to lower her eyes when we first met.

Her face had this secret charm to let people in. She had it in her body. She never tried to flirt with me Or tried to seduce me.

Her eyes didn't show me anything fake. Whenever I looked into her eyes she showed every emotion of care, love, and kind and she wouldn't have that look if she despised me.

Your eyes always show the emotion that you can never tell and I saw her but it was fake, all fake. Can I hate her?

Suddenly I hear gunshots going around the house. From every side of the house I hear gunshots, people screaming.

Might Rhyan be here? He's doing this to save me but I don't want to because this pain in my heart is breaking me badly.

I hear gunshots outside my room. I don't panic, I don't know why but this sound is making me feel good. People screaming, blood pooling outside my room, gunshots.

Tears start brimming in my eyes. This scene reminds me of my past which has been nothing but runaway for me.

A lesson to learn that not to trust anyone but I ignored it too. The door gets open and I see someone but can't recognise it as the tears are still there.

I'm feeling dizzy and I want to fall into that pit of darkness once again. Someone holds my face and pats my cheek.

Her rough hands were on my skin, her addictive scent lurking around me. Her face becomes clear and beautiful. Her eyes showed concern and worry in them.

"Zaeden.. Look at me. Are you okay? " She says but I can't hear her words properly. I touch her face as she opens my cuffs.

This is the woman I fell in love with and this is the same person that lied and played with me. I push her away from me as she backs away and falls. Her eyes again look at me in confusion in them.

She comes closer to me until someone comes inside the room. Sam. "Oh so finally you are here little sister. I have been waiting for you for so long. " He says.

"Back away Sam let Zaeden go and I'll give you anything. He didn't do anything. " She says keeping the in front of her.

"Oh yeah, you think. You started this game and I would like to end it as the only son of Vena Arnolds. " He says and comes forward.

He takes his knife out and plunges toward Lily as she defends herself. She still has her gun in her hands. She takes his knife and tricks him to his legs.

He falls beside me and screams. She devilishly looks at him. A smirk forms around her face as she looks at her injured brother.

Her eyes are showing nothing but a cold, deserted emotion in them. But her smirk faded which was starting to get my favourite.

She looks at me. Her eyes showed concern and love to me. She takes her gun and aims at me. I smile at her. A genuine loving smile.

My head is getting dizzy by the minute and I want to see her kill me. Her finger moves towards the trigger. Her face shows nothing but hatred for them.

I hear the gunshot. My eyes close. The headache going away. The tiredness I felt and the stinging pain in me is nowhere.

Is this how it feels to die at the hands of the person you loved when they didn't? Her face flashes in front of me.

Her face when she worksHer face when she is flusteredHer face when she is dancingHer face when she is angryHer cute little face in the morning She's laughing now She's smiling now Now she is hating me

I wanted to tell her how I feel about her, not when she is tired or angry. I wanted to tell her when she felt exactly what I felt for her.

But looks like I can never. Look Lily how you made me now. Vulnerable.

I will never forgive you and I'll hate you.

———————————

24.

Zaeden Carter

Is this how it feels to be dead by the love of your life or I thought that too.

I saw her entering the room and running towards me with tears, and worry in her eyes. Her face looked pale and dried.

Her face showed nothing but guilt, and worry. She knew that I had gotten to know about her little secret which she kept hidden from me.

I had this irritating headache for so long that I wanted to rip my head apart. Suddenly I heard someone talking.

I heard her. Her talking with someone.

"Rhyan if you don't drive fast I'm gonna lose my shit already. " She says. I'm in a car.

I feel her hands touching my face lightly with her rough hands. I flinch yet I feel some kind of relief.

Suddenly my body jerked to one side and a pain arose in my body. "Don't worry Zaeden we will be home soon. " I open my eyes slowly adjusting them to light.

Soon I see many people standing outside the car holding their guns and one of them is Lily. I look back and see none of the cars.

I get out of the car and walk towards Lily but before I can someone holds me back. "Sir, you can't get out of the car. " Rhyan says behind me.

"Leave it Rhyan let me go. " I say trying to get away from him. "Ms Knight said that whatever happens, you can't leave the car. " I look at him with a stunned face.

"So from when did you start listening to l- Ms. Knight? " I say cutting Lily's name. Suddenly gunshots go around.

Rhyan pushes me into the car. I look from the front window as everyone is hiding yet Lily is standing in between.

Oh, my fucking shit.

She just pulled a bullet through the man's head. She's just driving bullets through those people's heads. I get out of the car push Rhyan out of the way sit on the bonnet and look at the scene unfold before me.

It's fucking funny to say that I'm watching the woman I love fucking bullets into others head. I gather her every step moving ease yet calmness is in her body. Her face is out of emotions , darkness in her orbs.

She doesn't hide like the cowards are hiding and pulling bullets yet she is in open and it's clearly dangerous but she is dodging every bullet that passes her.

Suddenly a guy comes behind her and keeps a knife at her neck. As a trained woman she would be she catches his hand and pulls him forward putting the knife directly to his neck.

Suddenly she looks at me and gives me a wicked smile that means she's going to win everything. A smile needs to be cracked on my lips but everything Sam said playing In my head is a repeat to her deeds.

She's slicing every neck. A gunshot is heard I look in the direction and see Sam standing there with a bloody face.

He pulls his gun out and pulls trigger at her. The gunshot sound is clear to my ears. Everything gets silent, no one moves, no one talks.

I jump from the bonnet and look at Lily. She's crouched down and I can't figure out anything. I try to walk towards her but Rhyan stops me again.

"Sir please understand we need to leave. Ms Knight would kill me if anything happened to you. " He says stopping.

I hear a screeching laugh behind me. I turn back and look at the guy. "Finally after so long My lovely sister is dead. Dad would be so proud of me. Look at me now."

He walks towards her. Her body is still, the gunshot has pulled in her body. The blood is dropping from her body but I can't see any wounds.

"You know what Ms. Knight as how everyone says. " He looks at us. "This game of yours is now at an end and it's ended by Mr. Sam Arnolds the son of great Vena Arnolds. " He's still walking towards her slowly.

I jerk my body from Rhyan's hold but he stops me again. "Zaeden listen to me for once. " My eyes widen as he calls me my name. "Can't you see her? She's not dead, look at her hands. " He says.

I look at her hands as she holds a knife in her hand hiding it from Sam's eyes. "You know what because of you Dad never believed me because I was more like our stupid mother. But Dad wanted me to take his place as a cover for you so no one can know his tracks."

"But look where we are now? You dead and me alive and safe. You should have behaved nicely just like how you are. Yet I'm impressed with your defence skills as always you were ahead of me."

He's now standing in front of her and as he goes to bend down before he can she gets up and holds his neck and pushes him back to the car.

"Even if you dream about it let it be natural Sam. You just know the part of your site and what you've seen. It was hard for me too, way more than you." She huffs.

"I was a side piece, Sam, you were just for the show to lure them and don't tell me that dad's gonna make you the head because that's not gonna happen, he has decided Mr Rave as the head." Sam's face gets pale and he looks heartbroken.

"I wanted to tell you but you didn't believe me and the reason for exposing wasn't because I was angry 'cause he wanted to put you into trafficking Sam." Her hands loosen and he drops down to the ground.

"You're not alone Sam fucking Arnold. Well, I missed you too." He looks up and smiles at her."I fucking missed you too, knowing that you won't be there when I wake up in the morning."He hugs and whispers more words to her.

Everything gets confused, a few minutes before they were fighting and now they are hugging and smiling in reunion.

Suddenly his head snaps to mine and his eyes show rage in them. He taps on her shoulder and looks at me and then I see them.

The Sinister smile of hers.

She stands up with her brother and looks at me and her hand goes to her back. I follow her movements and see her hand coming back with a ..... gun.

She lifts the gun and points it at me. "Your time's over, while you did nothing but part us. This is where it ends Mr...."

Is this where it ends? Lily would kill me with her brother on the side and Ken would be supporting her. I die by the hands of the woman I love.

I look at her brother and see that he's shaking with anger, his veins popping out. "Fucking Arnolds." And a gunshot goes behind my ear.

I look behind and see that a body is lying down. The body of Vena Arnold. "We did it." I look at them. " We did it, Lily!" Sam says opening his arms towards her.

"It's not over yet I just killed the partner of this operation I still have the gang remaining." She replies lightly holding his face between her hands.

She pulls out her phone and calls someone." Ken, it's over!" She beams lightly in the phone.

Ken.

"Just send a backup and a car, we have Sam too just send him to my apartment. Yeah," she hangs up and gives him the phone.

"Sir, sir " I can't hear anything. All the voice from my body drains out. Rhyan comes in front of my view.

I hear cars pacing around and some people piling around us. I see her walking towards me with a smile. My heart breaks at the moment knowing that she has used me for her own business.

When she comes around and tries to touch my face, I push her back.

Lily Rose

He pushes me away when I come to touch him. I was craving his touch for so long that me needy. Not for his body but for his warmth.

He embraced me and told me sweet dirty words. Yet he pushes me away. "Zaed-" he cuts me off with his hands.

"You know what Lily you're such a liar. Everything's a lie. Your name, you're life and what more. You lied about everything so that you could use me for whatever you're a sting operation." He says his body is Shaking with pure anger.

" A sting operation? Seriously? Oh, so like we were having fun, right? You had this plan to seduce me, trap me, get out information and go away without a trace right?." Just looking at him is breaking my heart. He looks betrayed.

"And yes, I did fall into the trap and you ran away with whom? Ken the dumbass." He says and my blood boils.

"You don't get to say anything about him Zaeden," I reply. Ken has never harmed me. I know his feelings about me and he knows the correct answer to it. He never forced me into anything.

"Oh so now you're going to defend him, Lily." He says with sarcasm. I inch closer to him and say.

"He was and is a saviour to me. He saved and helped me when there was no one there. He was there for me and I know that he has feelings for me but he kept it to himself and never made me uncomfortable around him." He looks at me and scoffs.

"But you did run away, right? Tell me what you got from me, what details and people do I know that are into this?"

"Stop Zaeden stop please," I beg as my legs give up and tears fall down my face. We are far away from people so no one can hear us.

"I didn't seduce you Zaeden, it was never meant to happen this way. I was going to hack your files and all and you made me a contract with 3 years well it didn't matter much because it would be more easier for me." I sniff as more tears drop.

"But as I saw you, everything came down." "Yeah because I was enchanted with you so it could-." He replies

"I'm not done yet Zaeden," I say wiping my tears and standing up. "I didn't know that you were going to be there and I would meet you again at Chris's house and before it starts Chris doesn't know anything about me and he wasn't a stack." Before he would jump to any assumptions.

"But it started going differently and I didn't decline Well Ken did but I didnt listen to his words slowly we started growing closer and all with your teases." I smile when I remember all the moments.

"Yeah because it was easy to grab on me as I was liking you and you gave in because you felt good and all?" I scoff at his words.

This man doesn't get it. Men are dumb.

"No, I didn't give in because I wanted pleasure or because we can get closer and all. I gave in because...."

"Because what Lily?" He spits in anger.

I walk closer to him until I'm standing in front of him. The sun looks down on us as the wind passes through awakening my hair.

"Because I have started to fall in love with you."

———————

25.

Z aeden Carter

"Because I have started to fall in love with you." I swallowed the lump in my throat as my closed.

The wind passed us as our breathing could be heard. In the middle of nowhere, we are standing, just coming out of the mess.

I opened my eyes as I looked at her petite figure before me. She was standing in her glory, still a mess but beautiful. There's blood on her leather suit which shows her curves.

Her hair flowed with the wind as her lips trembled, her gaze locked with mine.

Fuck with this shit.

I ran towards her as she did the same. Our bodies collided with each other as tears flowed down. My hands snaked around her waist as her hands went to my neck and hugged her.

It was hard for her too but she still came. She came back to me. We pulled out as I wiped her tears which still streaming down her cheeks.

Our eyes crashed with each other as if on cue my lips crashed on her. Her hands went to my hair as I pulled our bodies closer.

Our lips moved against each other, words were poured out through the kiss. Those words which meant just for me as I had to know them. Every emotion poured out as our lips moved in sync.

How much had I missed her? But yet I didn't know the woman before was Blue Knight.

Well everyone thought she would be a man but she turned out to be a woman. She had a secret operation catching Sex traffickers.

Every human would lose their damn legs hearing her name. She is not just a woman but a fucking mastermind.

Never left a piece of trail behind her to let others know about her. Even I didn't get a piece of knowing that she already knew me.

She pulled out. Her breathing was uneven, her hair damp and her eyes turned a bit greenish as sunlight trapped her.

"You knew right?" I asked curious as I walked closer to her.

"About what?" She asked not sure of anything I was asking her about.

"The first time we met at the bar." She snapped towards me as the words left my mouth.

She nodded her head lightly. " I did know but I didn't purposely bump into you. I didn't even know that she was going there to sell me to you. " She said.

"But why? What's all this about ?" She never told me the real reason why this all has been happening.

"I'll tell you everything Zaeden I promise but now I need to go. Ken's waiting for me. " She says as she backs away. My jaw clenches. I take long strides towards her.

"Why is it always end with him? You belong to me and get that thing inside your head. " I say as her mouth shuts back. She nods her head and takes a step back.

"I'll meet you again Zaeden Carter. Wait for me. " She turns around and goes back.

I stand there and I can't do anything. I can still see her eyes on me as she talks with Rhyan. Her eyes collide with mine as she talks with Rhyan.

Her eyes move to her lips as her sentence ends. 'Take care of him while I'm not here and let him be happy. I'm not sure if I can come back. '

She turns around and walks back to her car I see Ken coming out of it. He walks towards Lily and takes her in his arms. Then he looks at her and asks something probably about if she is okay and all.

She goes towards Sam hugs him and exchanges more words with him and then she takes out something from her pocket hands him a gun and a knife turns around walking back to the car.

Then he makes her sit inside the car and for one last glance she turns around and mouths to me. 'Take care. '

I stand there still doing nothing to stop her because every word that is left on her lips is not coming out of my mind. My eyes meet Ken as his lips tug upwards in a cunning smile.

He's taking her away from you. Go stop her!

My legs work and I see myself walking towards the car but before I can reach it goes away. She left me again alone in this world.

"So. " My ears perk up as I hear the voice. I turn around and see her brother Sam standing there. Did she leave him behind alone?

" I know what you're thinking. She didn't, I needed to wait for another car. She is the best person ever can I think of. She took care of me in need because Dad knew I wasn't a person who could do all this.

He just named me as his heir and used me as bait. The real mastermind was her. She had planned out everything. She made Dad believe that she wanted to be a part of Sex trafficking.

But she just had to learn all about the people and tricks so she could use them against them. She wanted to be a bit better person. " He sighs as he walks toward me.

"And I know what she's doing is just to save those little children and women who were trapped into this shit. I can't tell you anything but I'll let you know.

She doesn't betray anyone, not those whom she loves and I saw it in her eyes after these long years. She had to suffer a lot Zaeden. " He sighs again showing that his tired.

"Do you want me to drop you?" I ask and then remember that he had nowhere to stay. " You can live in my house."

He looks at me and chuckles. "You thought Lily wouldn't have arranged a place for me? Like seriously dude? I thought she had a better taste in men but you're more than dumb. "

I scoff at his words. " As if. I'm more than in shock with what's happening around me and I'm still in a daze to let things accept me. I just didn't think about it. I'm not dumb. "

"Fine big man you can give me a ride I'll let her know. " He says and turns around. "Wait! " I say and walk towards him. "Where is Lily going? "

"I have no idea about that. My dad had let people know that he had caught the Blue Knight man and people were finding her like crazy around the state. So Ken might've arranged something for her. " He shrugs.

"I hate this Ken guy every time anyone says about him. " I say. "Yeah, you should because they would be together and might do some crazy shit. " He says and chuckles.

"Do you have his number and Or anything I can find him? I'll kill that bastard if he touches my women. " I say as I crack my knuckles.

"You love her, don't you? " He asks as I look at him. "She's more than that. " I say smiling at the memory of her.

"Come on lover boy drop me at her apartment. " He says and sits inside the car. I go inside the car and sit too.

"And what about the lady that Lily's been living with? " I ask at the memory. " That woman had lost her memory when her daughter had died. Lily had a perfect chance but that woman was more than crazy to let her treat like a maid.

But Lily still had a chance as she slept early in the nights so she could continue her oppression. Lily has gone through many shits. "

"She had a lot to endure. To let Dad trust her he had told her to kill our mother with her hands." He sighs looking down at the ring on his index finger and that same ring on Lily's hand too.

"So she killed? " I ask not wanting to bring the memories but letting them out for being curious.

He looks at me and smiles sadly. "She had to. Mom had spent her days with us smiling and letting us fill our empty capsules to remember her in every action of her life. She was already tired with her life.

Dad had abused her and used her as nothing but plastic. She had begged Lily to kill her so she could die peacefully. I still remember Mom's face when Lily held her trembling gun on our mother's head. Her first kill was our mother.

She pulled the trigger while closing her eyes and then she smiled at Mom's lifeless body. Her lifeless body smiling beautifully." His smile might be recovering the image of his mother.

"First time in her life I saw her smiling like that as if the whole world belonged to her. " He says looking at me. "And I'll kill you if you break that smile on her face and I'll wipe you out of this world. "

I smile at him. He gets out of the car as we reach her apartment. "It was nice meeting you Mr. Carter but still in a wrong way. " He chuckles.

"Likewise to be said, we'll meet again Mr. Arnolds. " I say but he stops me. "No, it's Mr. Rose. Shit that's more than bad. I should've told her to choose a nice last name. " I smile at him.

"Well what are you gonna do here anyway? " I ask. "Well I have company and he's called Chris as you know him very well. " My mouth opens in shock.

"You know him? "

"Of course, he had lived with Lily for a whole damn month. " He says

"Fine I'll leave you can call me if you need anything urgent and necessary. " I turn around and leave.

She has gone through many things in her life more than anyone could think of. It's a shit that she had to kill her parents to gain the trust. Then she plays the role of a daughter who is like a maid invisible from the world. Even a lot doesn't take place.

"Where are we going? " I ask as I see an unfamiliar road. "Sir Ms Blue - I mean Lily had arranged a house for you for a time being. "

Sighing I take a deep breath as I remind myself about the hectic day. My eyes widen as I see a house - more of a mansion. Guards everywhere I could see.

It's guarded heavily. I walk out of the car. I'm welcomed with Adri standing there. "Adri what you doing here?" I ask shocked with her.

"I don't know they just brought me here and said you're here. " She says and lets me inside the house.

"What's happening here Zaeden? " She asks disappointed with the situation.

"I don't know Adri. " I sigh. "Where's Lily? "

"I'll find her no matter what. I'll wipe out the world for her. "

———

26.

Z aeden Carter

"You little punks wake your ass up or mom's going to kill us all. " I groan as I hear Sam's voice. "I need to sleep for five more minutes man. " Chris says beside me.

"If you guys don't come in down in ten minutes you guys won't be getting the breakfast. " I hear mom scream from downstairs.

"But I still don't understand how many people are going to call her mom when she only has one child. " A chuckle leaves my mouth as Chris says.

"Well, that's not my fault that you're jealous. It's her who said to call me mom when I said, Mrs. Arden. " Sam says as he nears the bed.

"You know what you guys look like the couple you know legally tangled, almost naked. Lily would be devastated to see this when she's not here. " My eyes open automatically when hearing her name.

Lily.

My Lily.

"I miss that goddamn lady-man. What a fucking person she is." I smile hearing about that. " I can't even believe it's been a year since I have seen her. " My Lips tug downwards.

"You know that sneaky smile of hers when she's going to do something crazy or her being utterly clumsy and the movie nights that were the craziest. " Sam laughs as he imagines what Chris said.

"I don't have much to remember because all she had to do was to train herself every day but still at night she would come and keep a chocolate below my pillow when dad had beaten me. " Sam sighs.

"Do you have any idea where she is or what she is doing? " Chris asks as he sits up. " Nope." The only answer leaves from Sam's mouth.

"Then Ken's doing well hiding her. " Chris says as I lean my head to bed rest. "Correction Ken never hides. It's all a game plan. " Sam says. " What do you mean by that? " Chris asks.

"Ken is the person who handles every step of Lily and gives her the next step but the main mastermind is Lily the one who handles everything. If Lily wanted she could have come back. " Sam says shrugging his shoulders.

"What do you mean if she wanted to? " I ask. "I mean she may have come back but might she had any mission or something? " Sam says clearly understanding the point of me being eagerly curious.

"Well, you guys should get freshen up if you don't want another lecture. " I sigh fed up with this conversation.

"I'll use the other bathroom, you can use this. " Chris says as he leaves the room with Sam. I nod not knowing what has to leave my mouth.

It's been a year, a fucking year of waiting for her. I'm tired of waiting, I'm tired of imagining her smile, her fragrance which doesn't even linger in my mind, I just remember how she used to look.

I don't even know how she's been doing or how she is. What's happening with her or if she is alive or any fucking thing.

"Zaeden are you coming down or not either way I'm coming to grab your ass. " I shake my head trying to lighten up my head even though I know it's not going to work.

"Mom, is that even language? " Chris scolds. " Excuse you, my son, I'm your mother for a goddamn reason and you don't get to teach me that when I know what you guys have been doing. "Chris's mom says.

I make my presence downstairs as Chris's mom stops scolding Chris and looks at me. "Good morning to you. " She smiles at me as she sets everything on the table.

"Good morning Mrs. Arden. " Sam beams at her as she eyes on him. " I've said this before too. " Mom says as Sam starts. "Well, your son is jealous because we all have been calling you 'Mom'. " Mom starts laughing as everyone looks at Chris who's denying yet not saying anything.

"It can happen when I have such awesome lads in my house. " Mom beams at everyone. "Hey! Am I missing something? "Chris's dad asks as he presents himself.

"Well you did uncle, you did needed to see WellChris's face reddening in embarrassment because he doesn't want anyone to call his mother 'Mom's. "Chris's dad laughs as he looks at the messy people on the table.

He walks towards Chris's mom and places a kiss on her temple as she smiles at him. Everyone sits at the table waiting for the delicious breakfast made by the mother.

"Here comes the awaiting breakfast of the day made by My mom. " Chris says giving us a little glare as he walks beside his mother. "For her children and her lovely husband. " He completes his sentence.

"Come on guys, eat the breakfast we can have later coming in too. "

"Zaeden have you found out about the woman, Lily? " Dad asks and I feel everyone's eyes on me. I exhale loudly shaking my head.

After everything happened I came back to this house as Rhyan had told me. Everyone had to shift here for their safety.

Everyone asked Chris what was happening because still everyone believed that she was his girlfriend. I had to settle everyone down to let them know that Chris wasn't sharing any relationship with her.

Well, more than anything Chris's mom was beyond shocked about it she said "That means Lily is not going to be a part of us, I liked her more than anything. I'm going to kill you, Chris. "

It was shocking but later when she got to know that I was being with her she was ecstatic. "At least one of my sons got to be with her. "

At first, it was a bit difficult to get comfortable with this place as time went by everyone enjoyed it. Sam was more engaging with us as the time left.

Everyone felt more at ease and it didn't even feel a bit threatening. People weren't allowed inside the house unless it was urgent for them they had to be seated in the garden.

Guards weren't anywhere to be seen but I knew they were there standing in their glory to save us. Lily had made our family grow back together.

Every morning it's filled with laughter and at night it ends with sneaky giggles. We all have been living in fun as a family should live.

It's hard to not remember her when I know she's doing this for my sake so that I won't remember her or maybe forget her.

I know she's still there thinking about how am I doing and all. Somewhere she is wanting to get back to me but it's the world trying to separate us from each other.

Today I'm going to do the same and she would also appreciate me for that, I know it feels a burden to her but I'm going to make it easier for her.

"Hey buddy what have you been thinking about? " The voice of Chris wakes me up from my daydreaming thoughts.

"Nothing serious. " I say keeping my point out to them. "What have you thought? "Chris's mom asks. I look up to meet everyone's gaze planted on me.

"About what? " I ask to know what they are talking about. "It's been a year Zaeden a year. There's no contact or even a text about her. No one knows where she is not even her goddamn brother.

You need to do something Zaeden Or at least get to know where she is, what she is up to. " Chris says. I glance at Sam as he nods his head to the back.

"I'm sorry guys I need to attend a call. " Sam says and walks into the backyard. "Do you think Sam doesn't have any contact with Lily like even a bit maybe a text or might he have a burner phone? " Chris asks.

"I don't think that Chris, you know it's not easy to get a burner phone. " I say. "You don't know Zaeden Lily has a big-. " He stops knowing that if the sentence ends there's going to be a questionnaire.

"Lily has a big what? "Chris's mom asks as she gets curious about the talkative. Chris glances at me knowing I'm the only one to stop it at the moment.

"There's no Lily big he just wants to excuse himself, Mom. Stop excusing yourself, Chris. " I say.

"But still I never understood why she left or what she's been doing. You guys gave me the explanation but it's still not enough. " She says taking her and her uncle's plate.

"Don't worry Mom there's nothing to know about. " I say giving my dirty plate to the maid. "What do you mean? " Chris ask.

I stand up and walk myself not wanting them to listen to the words that are going to leave my mouth. I see Sam standing beside the pool.

"I know that you have thinking about this for so long and it's been hectic for you too. " Sam says as I near him.

"I have decided and today I'm going to do what I have been planning for messing with my nights," I say sadly smiling.

"What have you thought? " Sam asked worried for me.

"I'm going to do what Lily might be proud of. Today I'm going to stop waiting for her and move on."

"Are you sure Zaeden? " He asks me.

"Yes." The only answer I could afford.

"She would happy Zaeden because she's stresses herself too easily and she has never left anyone behind until you. " He pauses and looks at me and smiles.

"I know you're doing this for her sake and I know it would be hard but less stressful. I'll give her your message.

I smile sadly and give him a last glance before walking out.

––––––––––

The trees and bushes pass by my car as drive towards the destination. My car halts at the destination that has been on my mind ever since.

I open the door and close it behind me. The fresh air fills my nostrils but the memories play in my head.

I walk ahead to meet the fantasized place that's been playing on my head keeping me up for countless nights.

The sound of crashing water reaches my ear as I smile at it. Our first time being out embarrassingly almost naked.

I smile at the vivid memory as it replays in my mind. This was the last place I could think to say goodbye to her.

I know it won't reach to her but it will reach to my heart that's once owned by her and it still does when I say those last words to her.

I walked to the other side and walked where I could reach my destination. The leaves leave an unexpected feeling to me.

I'm saying goodbye to her and I hope she forgets me while I try to because I know I never would be able to leave her behind.

She left a beautiful piece of her with me, a burning lingering touch on my body whenever she touched me.

It's hard it's fucking hard to leave a person whom you have started to love fuck that shit I already damn love her.

Suddenly my nostrils fill with a familiar scent that I have been longing for. I close my eyes in defeat.

It is playing tricks with you. It's not her, you know it because she can't come back to me.

I walk ahead feeling the leaves leave a frustrated sound beneath my shoes. I walk fast keeping my face down.

I feel the fresh air hit me and a sudden wave of familiarity is felt. It's not something I always have felt. I'm mostly lonely over here.

It's my property and no one means not any other human being is allowed over here.

Until a wave of a familiar scent hits my body and my body on its own finds its way.

My breath is uneven, my body shaking and my mouth running dry as I feel a rush of blood losing my body.

My eyes widen in shock as I near the cliff. A woman is sitting down, her hair long, black and wavy. The wind shuffles as her hair moves in sync with the air.

My body is shaking, out of breath and I can't seem to do anything afraid if I lose sight.

Her face turns towards me as I see the familiar features of her and her eyes meet mine. Our eyes collided and her lips moved as I heard words leave her mouth.

" A goodbye isn't easy to say, Right Zaeden?"

_____

27.

Zaeden Carter.

The busy life I had was everything a normal working man would have. Just working, working and working...

It's easy when people give you interest which makes your ego bigger and have rich dude-ass money just have nothing to worry about.

Until my eyes laid on a woman who had abruptly from nowhere had bumped into me making my emotions go over my head.

You know what, I would have killed that person to just meddle in my way but why?

But why did I stop? Why didn't I tell Rhyan to kill her? Why did my body had stopped it's sense to work for a second?

Why there's a way to everything?

Because I saw her in a black slutty dress which did match her curvaceous body but not her emotions. Her black eyes were something that triggered me.

Her attitude towards me had made me all gone. Her beauty and the way her lips moved to speak.

Fuck.

I felt it the damp heart of mine had worked up in years. I don't know why but it beat again when I saw her again in the room with her mother.

Why?

Because you fell in love the moment you laid it.

Did I? She knew her stepmother or whatever's intention. Ken was helping, they had a mission planned so was this planned too?

But does it mean she can't love me? No, of course not I have seen it when she said those three words to me. Which I have been longing to hear from her.

Was it wrong for us to fall in love? A sinful man and a woman who was killing people to save the lives of children and women. In the world of sex trafficking, Lily was paving her way.

She had made people go back to their normal life of living even if it triggered them yet they had gotten a chance to live.

A chance was given back to them so they could live and rebuild their future instead of being owned and sold.

A trafficking ring was something people were not aware of or didn't have any interest in but it was the biggest thing to let a human life be compared with money.

A human's life and soul were being sold for a token of notes.

And a year passed with me leaving her behind and moving forward but why was I back?

Did my instincts know this? I had come here to say my least and last words to Lily Rose as she had been nowhere to know.

But here she was standing at the end of the cliff as the sun dipped behind her, the wind making her short hair work.

Her cheeks were scratched. My eyes moved down as I saw her body. Scratches, cuts, and scars were drawn into her body. My eyes moved up to her burning eyes.

But her eyes shined as she saw me and her lips curved into a smile.

Her lips moved to form a sentence as I heard her angelic voice.

" A goodbye isn't easy to say, Right Zaeden?"

My heart stopped working, my eyes closed on their own as I listened to the words. Her voice wasn't good because it felt distant as those words reached my ears.

I came here for the last time so I would stop loving her and move on with my life but why did it feel so wrong from her side?

My eyes opened as I looked at her, she was smiling as she looked at me. Tears prickled at her iris as they swore to spill yet she kept her smile on her face, a genuine smile.

I inched closer to her as her smile lifted more. "Didn't Ken give you any food or something?" The words left before I could think.

Her laugh landed on my ears as my lips tugged upwards. "Is that a even question you ask a person you meet after so long?" She asked me.

I answered back "Look at yourself it looks like you haven't been sleeping or eating anything. " She smiled as she walked until she stood in front of me.

Her hands slipped to my cheeks as she lightly massaged them her eyes bore to mine and I leaned into her touch.

"I missed you, I missed you goddamn so much." Her tears fell down her cheeks as she said. I smiled lightly.

We both knew to the point we both missed each other like crazy. "A hell of a crazy year I passed without you," I said.

"I didn't even feel when a year passed without you Zaeden. I was so engrossed in the business."

"I missed you too Lily. I was crazy to a point that you won't imagine." I said as she smiled.

My hands moved towards her waist as I pulled her closer to me leaving no gap between us.

My eyes were mixed with her as I leaned down and connected our lips. She smiled in between the kiss as I deepened the kiss.

I pulled her closer and ate her lips. She gasped as I squeezed her buttcheeks and inserted my tongue riding her mouth in deepness. She hummed as her hands buried in my hair.

Few minutes which felt too surreal to be alive as our lips collided with each other in the acceptance of meeting each other again after a year.

She lightly tapped my shoulder as I kissed her for the last time. She smiled taking my hands in her non-comparable short hands.

She walked until we were on the end of the cliff. She sat down keeping her legs at the end. I sat behind her still looking at her as she looked at the scenery.

Her eyes beamed with rejoicing and then they moved to mine as she smiled heartedly. I pulled her closer until she was on my lap.

"Where were you for this many times?" I asked as questions of question ran inside my head.

"I was in every other country you could name. " She smiled as she continued speaking." I got a new mission in Puerto Rico where women were going to be auctioned. And then I went to Florida as children were being kidnapped. California, France, Russia, India."

"Many of the things happened in a year I lost my asshole of a dad and people were still behind and thankfully my dad didn't let them know that it was his daughter who ruined his hardworking shit business or his name would have gotten into deeper shits." She continued as she played with the hem of her dress.

"We had to change our place because people were getting to know about me. Ken helped me a lot with this to keep me discreet. " She sighed as her mouth opened but no words spilled out.

I smiled cupping her cheeks as I looked into her eyes. I kissed her nose, cheeks, eyes and then the lips. A chuckle left her lips.

"How did you know I was going to come here?" I asked because that was the first question I had to ask.

"I knew that one day you would come here in the memory of us. I saw you leaving so I thought to give you a surprise." She said lightly brushing her fingers through my hair locks.

I frowned at her answer." What do you mean that you saw me leaving?" I asked confused.

"I have cameras all around the house and the guards and maid would report me whatever happened there. "

"You would be awake and exercise at late night. You wouldn't even eat until Chris's mom didn't slap your ass. And my most trusted person Sam was letting me know whatever you do.

If any person would go out of the house the guards would be following them but not too obvious. No one was allowed inside the house until I approved them."

I was shocked to hear this. She knew " I was keeping a watch on you guys even if I was far away I was still close. " Without any further I kissed her

I kissed her, I kissed her like I owned her. Her hands wrapped around my neck as my hands went to her hips pulling her closer.

Her dress had risen showing her long legs, I pulled her closer as I couldn't control myself.

Lily Rose.

His lips landed on mine as my hands reached his neck, silently urging him to kiss me back,

His warm breaths were heavy as they mingled along with mine, the skin of his neck was damp, warm- from the beads of perspiration that were beginning to form.

His lips tasted sweet and tangy- probably from the apple juice he had earlier in the morning.

Silent pleas resonated within me as I felt a whisper of a breeze floating through, my heart palpitating abnormally fast.

The throbbing between my legs got more prominent as I clenched my thighs together, hoping to relieve the ache between them.

His breathing was laboured, I could feel the singular vein in his neck throbbing under my skin.

His smell was overwhelming, overpowering and nurturing my senses, adding fuel to the fire that had been burning for a long time.

A shaky breath escaped me as I pressed my body to his, deepening the kiss, a strangled moan escaping me as I relished his taste. My toes curled from the pleasurable sensation.

He was so fucking handsome. I could feel his lips touching my skin as he feathered it on my skin. He held me roughly, yet I could feel that he was holding back.

"St-Stop teasing me," I mewled, silently begging him to fuck me here, at the end of the cliff.

"Do you think you deserve to be fucked? You have been away from me for 14 months."

I moaned in frustration. He was playing with me and he knew exactly what he was doing.

I was on the verge of exploding, I could feel my wetness as I sat on his lap.

"P-Please.."

"Fuck it," His soft curse was all I heard before his lips descended mine, capturing it in a hasty but rough kiss, "Tell me to stop."

His lips began kissing down my neck and to my collarbone. My toes curled as I threw my head back, my fingers threading through his silk strands as I silently coaxed him to stop with his games already.

I felt his teeth nibbling on the skin of my neck. A loud moan escaped me as I felt myself on the verge of losing my sanity.

He pulled back and I took in his features hungrily. Even at the most intimate of moments, he was in control.

I took his hand that gripped my chin, grabbing his finger and gently sucking it in between my lips. Wrapping my tongue around it, I sucked it into my mouth, hollowing my cheeks, just as I would to a cock.

His other hand tugged my hair painfully, yet it only added to the raw pleasure I was feeling. He ran his wet digit along my lips, tracing it painfully slow, shutting me off.

"Take off your dress, Lil cat" His command was harsh, and brief and I didn't need to be told twice. I lifted my hips and took it off in a go.

"Keep your eyes on me, if they aren't already," I looked at him, panting heavily as he licked the fingers that had been in my mouth. I felt a gush of wetness as I watched his tongue slowly lick them, wetting them further.

I moaned, turned on to a point where there was no going back. His smell invaded my senses, along with the scent of my arousal. It was a heady mixture.

His grip on my hair tightened as he slammed two of his fingers into my pussy, making my back arch.

A cry escaped me as I felt the pain seeping in with the pleasure.

felt his other hand grip the back of my hair as he drove his finger further into my mouth almost touching the back of my throat.

I was seeing stars behind my lid. I was so close to breaking, yet so far. I was fulfilled, yet I needed more. Sparks ran along my skin as my mouth fell agape. I took his intimidating form through my blurred vision.

His hand left my neck, and he trailed his fingers along the hem of my blouse, making me squirm impatiently.

"You are making a mess," He smirked, "All over my fingers."

Oh. God.

He was playing me like a marionette on strings and I was losing my damn mind. A sob escaped me as one of his fingers lowered my blouse, exposing my large breasts.

"Please-" I sobbed, "Please I can't ta-"

I was transcending, on the verge of an orgasm- every single bit of me was ready to explode. I was creaming all over him like a bitch in heat.

He pinched each of my swollen nipples, making me cry out in pain and my breasts bounce. The sensitivity of which turned into pleasure. I bit my lips, to prevent myself from screaming the cliff down.

I gasped from the sharp sting throwing my head back, tears cascading down as I saw bursts of colors behind my lids, my back arching.

"You're fucking beautiful," he murmured before he wrapped his lips around one of my nipples.

I cry out, wondering if people could hear me.

His mouth was flaming, he nibbles on the sensitive spot before licking and sucking it- soothing the ache.

"Zae- Zaeden. "

He retracts his fingers from inside my cunt immediately, making me whimper at the loss.

"Another word, Lily" he uttered, menace lacing his voice, "I am going to leave."

I clamped my mouth shut.

He returned his attention to my breasts, biting, licking, sucking; occasionally pinching until I cried out loud. I was helpless underneath him and he hadn't even fucked me.

My clit throbbed painfully, begging to be touched and have a release.

He returned his attention to my breasts, biting, licking, sucking; occasionally pinching until I cried out loud. I was helpless underneath him and he hadn't even fucked me.

He brought his wet fingers up, which had been inside me a while ago, to my lips and commanded, "Suck."

I dart my tongue out, having a taste of myself on his fingers before wrapping my lips around his fingers.

All I saw was stars.

Our eyes met. The burning gaze of ours met each other under the sunset. I could see his brown orbs more behind the lust.

Our faces got inches closer, breathing ragged yet away from the bliss I got off now. His mouth clasped on mine. Forgetting the world behind us.

Our lips were tangled in each other's embrace as we found ourselves. We found the real meaning of what was left behind.

He was a sinner and I was the saviour, a sinner I would like to kill and leave a good purpose behind yet that didn't happen.

It's couldn't happen. I was taken into the arms of the devil and exposed to a world that I didn't belong in. With a desired thirst and need for destruction, our demons danced, and I lost myself

I lost myself in him.

And now, I'm found... we both are.

----

28. .

☐ ▢▢▢▢ ▢▢▢▢

The familiarity hit me as I took a step inside the big mansion. My heart started beating again as I saw Chris on a call upstairs.

I looked beside me as I felt a cold yet warm hand on my waist. I smiled looking at him.

Zaeden was there standing beside me smiling. After our little Intense day at the end of the cliff, we decided to come back and greet everyone.

I was so excited to meet everyone but felt guilty about leaving without anything. I looked up and called out.

"Chris!" His face never moved so fast, he might have hurt his neck. His eyes went big as he saw me.

He ran downstairs saying "Lily, oh my gosh." He didn't stop until his body met with mine. he hugged me close to his body.

My eyes welled up with tears as he cupped my cheeks with his warm palms. He looked at me and smiled.

"Fuck Lily do you even know how much I missed you. I mean oh gosh is that you?" He asked disbelief at the fact I was standing in front of him.

I nodded as my tears fell down my cheeks. He hugged me again and whispered "I love you oh god this year was so hard without you. I have many teas to spill too." He said making me chuckle.

"I missed you too Chris," I said as more tears fell. "Oh my gosh! Is that Lily?" I heard someone say as I recognised the voice.

I looked back and found Chris's mom standing there with her hand on her mouth as she gasped looking at me.

"Oh my gosh, Lily is that you? Is that gosh my-." She said coming closer to me as her hands wrapped around me.

My eyes were burning with tears. I had many scenes in my head dancing as I thought about how I felt and what emotions would blast as I saw everyone's face.

But the real feeling can never be expressed in words. And now I'm feeling hundreds of emotions as everyone's face is visible.

She suddenly pulled back and scanned me from up and down. Then her brows frowned and she looked at me.

"Didn't you eat anything these days? Look at you. " I looked down at me and then at her.

"Oh, my god Lily you have lost so much weight come on let's eat. " She took my hands in her as I walked with her.

I turned behind and looked at Zaeden and Chris as they both giggled at me. My head hit something as I looked up and found mom looking behind me.

"You guys bring your ass to the kitchen and help me out. " She said and walked ahead. As I started walking something hard came down my butt.

Chris had spanked me. Hard.

"What the fuck Chris? " I asked bewildered. He smirked at me as his hand came to my waist holding me close. "What's with that grin? " I asked slightly suspicious.

"You're going to be dead baby. " He whispered in my ear. My brows grew in confusion. "What does that mean? " I asked.

"You know right Zaeden's been away from for a year? He was like a crazy dude, I mean he got angry about the slightest things and he was a big ass in our butt. " I laughed as he spoke ahead.

" But the main was he never went to meet any women he didn't even to clubs, and right now he's ridiculously jealous seeing us like this. "

My eyes widened as I realised how close we were standing his hands on my waist and his head leaning to my ear. And then the worst thing he did.

He kissed me on the cheek and then on the forehead. He stopped and smirked badly. He turned around with me as his words spoke. " Zaeden aren't you coming? "

My eyes widened as my gaze landed on Zaeden. He wasn't looking at me rather he was looking at the hand wrapped around my waist. Chris understood.

He pulled me closer to his body. I looked at Chris and tried to push him but it didn't work. I heard footsteps coming closer to us.

My eyes returned to him and his gaze belonged to mine. Deep, dark sinister eyes looking into my soul. I still knew this look from a year back.

"I-" Before I could even say a word he moved ahead to the kitchen. I looked at Chris as he kept his lips thinned to stop his smile.

"Fuck you. " I exclaimed and moved forward. "Oh but wouldn't Zaeden help you with that? " I showed my finger to him and walked towards the kitchen.

I saw Mom working and went behind her. "Mom I'm not hungry you don't need to do this," I said as she glared at me.

"Look at you you were away for a year and what have done! " She exclaimed. "But I still missed you, everyone missed you. We talked about you every day. "

I smiled remembering the CCTV flashes in front of my eyes. "Can I help you?" I asked. "No, you might be tired. You little punks come here. "

Suddenly I felt someone behind me. I felt the familiar warmth behind me yet it felt distant. I turned around and my eyes found his.

My breath hitched. His eyes were deep, dark, sinister and mysterious. He was angry. Rage was dancing in his pupils.

He took a step toward me but before he could do anything a voice broke. " Zaeden oh can you get the veggies from the refrigerator? Chris! " She said.

He took a step back and walked towards the refrigerator. I was frozen in the place. Was I even breathing?

He took out the veggies and started walking towards me. His eyes bored into mine. His hand brushed through mine as he walked past me.

A shiver ran down my spine. "Thanks, Zaeden Can you cut these veggies and you? " She said to Chris as his steps lingered on the floor.

"Help with the stirring. " She said. I felt a hand snake to my waist. I looked down and found a huge veiny hand around my waist.

It pulled me forward, I looked at him and tapped his hand to leave me. He didn't look at me and walked until we were behind the mahogany table.

He kept the fresh washed-out vegetables on the table. He took out a knife from the drawer. He looked at me. My eyes went to his lips as a smirk stood proudly on his lips.

He took my hands into his and pulled me in front of him. He was behind me, his breath was fanning my neck making me feel vulnerable.

I felt his lips on my ear as he spoke barely a whisper. "Don't make a noise. Don't want Chris's mom to see this. " My eyes widened in fear.

"Za.. Zaeden you can't do this here. " I said while stuttering as I felt his tongue on my earlobe. I tried to push myself from the table but he pushed me more into the table.

My core was pressed onto the cold table side. "Shut your mouth like good girl you are lil cat. " The words left his mouth as my mouth dried up.

The word I have been longing for a year had slipped his mouth. This felt like a pain but yet it felt good. His mouth went to my neck as he left wet sloppy kisses there.

My teeth stop my lips to stop the nasty moans from moving out of my mouth. He licked the skin behind my ear and my breath hitched in place.

"How did you feel when he whispered like this? Did you like it? Did he make you feel like this, incapable?"

It was hard, hard for me to control when he spoke like this rough, angry, desperate, lust everything was in his voice.

His hand traced my arms, back and then the thigh. "Zaeden are you-. "
Hearing Mom's voice I take the knife on the side and push him back with
my butt.

"Lily? " I look up and smile awkwardly. She comes by our side and goes to
Zaeden. "You punk! I told you to cut it not her. She might be tired. Do it
Now!"

A smile erupts on my face as Chris sends a wink towards me. "I'm coming
back in a few minutes those should be done by then. "Chris's mom says.

"And you. " She points a finger at Chris. " Help me with carrying those bags
from the car. " She walks by as Chris follows her.

A breath leaves my body but before I can do anything his body collides
with mine as he turns my face to the side and kisses me.

He hungrily kissed my lips and I returned them equally. We were both
needy. Needy of each other, his hands, his lips, his warmth everything I
was needy for.

His hands moved down to my dress hem and lifted it. His cold hands met
my ass, he massaged them and then the hit came.

I was jerked ahead yet he still kept kissing me. A smile broke from my lips.
He left my lips with a plop sound.

His lips came behind my ears as he spoke."Don't worry baby somehow
those lips would be crying when I fuck you on this very table."

It felt like a sin when everyone was out there and anyone could come in and
see us but it felt more thrilling.

"Zaeden stop this-." He bit my neck as a moan slipped out. "You will keep
your mouth shut and cut those vegetables while I fuck you from behind."

My lips form into thin lines and I grasp the knife in my hand as his hands catch the line of my underwear.

He pulls it down and his hands go to my dripping wet core. "You are loving this don't you lil cat."

I heard his pants coming undone and nervousness grew up. His cock lines up at my entrance.

"Take that knife in your hands and cut those vegetables. You don't want to disappoint Mom right?" I shook my head.

My hands feel the cold handle of the knife as I take the carrot in my hand. A gasp leaves my mouth as he enters me. "Shh baby, a sound and leave the kitchen."

I try slicing up the carrots but it doesn't work as he moves Inside me. The sounds are stopped by the teeth.

I don't know how I cut those in really bad slices. He starts moving at a really fast pace and he makes me bend over the table.

He takes the knife and keeps it on my neck. I feel the cold blade of the knife grazes my skin. "How would it feel to have a knife on your neck and I'm fucking you. "

He comes closer to my ear and whispers. " Do you feel scared? " He presses the knife more into my skin. "I can kill you right away Lil cat and punish you. "

Fear? In this moment there's no fear for me. "Ahh." A whimper leaves my mouth as pinches my thighs. The knife is on my shoulder and he presses it more and I'm sure there's blood.

I feel it pierce my skin. "You're going to remember this every time you look at a mirror. " He says and fucks me. I feel the orgasm coming near and my legs shake.

"You want to cum Lil cat? " I nod my head in a desperate. " Say it. " My eyes open and I look at him.

"Say it if you want to cum. " He's still fucking me and I don't want to stop. After a year I'm getting fucked. I'm a woman with needs.

"Let me cum Zaeden. Fuck, please. " I don't know how loud I said that but now the skin-slapping sounds could be heard through the house.

" Fuck Lily. Cum. " I just need the words and I did. My body shakes as the orgasm leaves me. The knife moves on my arms as I wince in pain. "Zaeden!
"

The blood drips on the table as he puts the knife on the table. He pulls out of me puts the dress back and dresses himself. I turn around and glare at him.

"Are you Fucking sane?" I ask him as I touch the wound. The blood drips but he walks around and brings a tissue roll.

I snatch it and place it on my shoulder. "Why did you do it? " I ask. He comes closer as I take a step back to meet the table. " When someone touches you show it to them. " He moves back and leaves the kitchen.

"Did you cut the vegetables Zaeden? " I hear Mom's voice and turn around to look at the vegetables scattered around the table.

"Oh my gosh. " I look up to find Mom's shocked gaze. "That little punk can't even do that. " Then she looks at me. "Did you guys fight? He seemed to be angry."

"Oh my gosh, what happened to your hand? The blood is dripping out." she squeaks as she looks at my hand. " It's okay mom I just got a cut. You don't need to worry much."

"Did you guys fight? He seemed angrier." Mom says as she wraps the tissue.

I look down at the floor. " I don't know what happened but don't let him out angry. " I nod my head.

"Did you meet Sam?" I shook my head in denial. "You haven't met him too he's your brother. He might be in the garden. I just saw him there." She said as I nodded my head and walked towards the garden.

I open the door of the Lawn as my gaze tries to find Sam's. Just I see his figure standing at the end.

"Baa baa black sheep have you any guns for me? "

"Maybe if you would be early you would have gotten them. "

———————

29.

L ily Rose

"So do you have any guns for me? " I say as my eyes land on the familiar figure that I haven't seen for a year.

Hearing my voice he looked from his shoulder and smiled. "Yes li, yes li 1 pack of guns. " I laughed. "Just one? I thought we told each other selves that we should have at least 20."

"if I got any guns which means if I got any sour bears." I walked closer until I was beside him standing and looking at the scenery.

"Maybe my baby brother promised me he would bring me the 'guns' he was talking about when we met again. " His shoulders dropped as he sighed.

His hand went to his pocket and he took out a small pack of sour candies. A smile made it to my face. "You brought them? " I asked unsure of it.

He turned to me but didn't look at me instead he looked at the pack. "Do you remember this? " I nodded.

" You didn't want dad to know that you loved gummy bears so much that you needed to call them 'guns'. " Sam said as he smiled.

"The first ever time you left me alone on the bed because we had a fight about how gross of me to kill Maria and I couldn't sleep the whole night. " I looked down at sour packs as it brought the memories.

"Because you couldn't sleep and couldn't cry because dad would get to know that you're weak and he would replace me. " I smiled and looked at him.

" It was not how I was being responsible as a sister but because I had to kill our mother just to gain his trust. It was not just about you it was about how you would have to take responsibility and kill another human just to show that you're loyal and not weak. There was a lot more to that Sam."

"I don't fuckin' understand why you had to do this all. I mean, I don't give a fuck about this but did you look at yourself. You're tired, shit, exhausted and have you even been eating? " Sam asks as he walks closer to me.

"It doesn't matter now Sam. " I say as I look down. "It does Li, it does. Do you even know How worried I was for you? I mean we did talk but you just asked about how everyone has been and the guest details.

And mostly about Zaeden, I felt more guilty that I couldn't even tell him how you were getting through where you were. How you were? Nothing. "

Sam's words start getting into me as tears pick my eyes. "He was getting crazy, at first he wasn't talking with anyone, no one and wasn't even eating until Chris's mom took matters into her hands. And then suddenly he buried himself into work but still and at the end of the day he remembered you.

He didn't want anyone to talk about you it was like he wanted to hate you and do you even know why he went to that place so that he could stop loving you and then he was going to move away from us?

Even from Chris's parents, he was going to settle somewhere he would distract himself with nature and not be reminded by you. " He continues speaking.

"And in a year a lot has changed but one thing I know for sure and it's never gonna change. That Zaeden loves you a lot. "

I look at him as he smiles. "I thought he hated you because you had kidnapped him. " I smile. "He did but eventually he couldn't resist himself from my charms you know. " a laugh bubbles from my throat as he tries showing his charms.

I look down as guilt forms in my body. " I don't know what to say anymore. " He speaks " You have done the best any sister could do and for that, you don't have to apologize. "

A tear falls from my eyes as his words seem to be prepping up my emotions. "I'm sorry Sam, I'm sorry for what I did but I didn't have a choice. If I haven't gone away you guys would be in danger. "

He comes closer to me as speaks. " I know Li It's not your fault I don't blame you for that but maybe somehow a word would have done him better. "

"I know it's not your fault, you, me we've been through a lot but somehow we are at fault too. Zaeden didn't want anyone to have your name on their lips."

" I have no more words left to describe how guilty I feel for this, I can't describe how I feel right now. Mom has been acting like nothing has happened it's like I wasn't away for a year."

" Everything's changed Li, a lot has happened in a year and you weren't here to tell, or do anything I do understand but everyone has their thoughts on it. No one you've been through can understand our pain. A sob breaks from my lips as his hands warm me in a hug.

"It's okay Li no one's here to listen. No one is going to say that you're weak because you're not. Pour them out Li you're the best. " More tears fell from my eyes as I pent up my emotions which I have been holding up for years. His words make me feel more light.

"It has ended Li, no one's gonna hurt you anymore. "

Zaeden Carter

I don't know why but I still feel lonely yet. She's back but she hasn't said a word about it yet and what are we going to do with our relationship?

It's just taking a normal role in others. Mom's busy making her eat something and Chris is stuck between the kitchen and Me, I'm just roaming around trying to figure out myself.

Until I hit the balcony of the backyard. The balcony knows me the best because I have been the person who's been in and out.

Looking up at the sky as smoke pours out my lips and take little sips until my eyes burn to sleep. Somehow this balcony made me feel closer to her.

How she told me that she used to open her windows and give out her lungs because it made her feel lighter and away from the dark world yet it didn't bring me any warmth.

The cold winds breezing past me felt more colder to her. No calls, texts, letters no fucking shit and suddenly she's here and what did we even do.

Kiss and make up what they call here and we did just that without any understatement. I don't know if I should even talk with her.

I'm happy that she's finally back but now what? Is she going back again? Any more missions? Is she still going to work? why do I care so much? She didn't care about me so much.

I had my thoughts running everywhere, it was all over the place I don't know what the thoughts were but now when I think about it was me being selfish and foolish it was her job to protect children and women from being slaves, it was me being foolish to love her.

I don't know what love means to me but now maybe I know. It's foolish and selfish, kid type when you think it but somehow it makes my heart flutter to know that there's someone I know and I love her.

I can't feel it when she's standing with Sam and crying as he holds her in his arms whispering in her ear. It's heartbreaking when I see her crying, pouring out her emotions. I have never seen her crying but it's how it makes her strong and responsible.

I'm proud of her even if she didn't think about me but still, she has the power to make me love her all over again. Now I see Sam's smile back on his face as he looks at his sister and smiles wipes her tears as she smiles sadly.

I walk down the stairs and make my way towards the backyard. I have made my decision and now I just need to tell her and I need no permission from her. The glass door opens as I make my way towards them. Sensing my presence Lily's gaze runs over me.

Her once sad gaze brightens as she lightly smiles but I don't give her satisfaction of my smile. I look at Sam as if he senses my intention of privacy with her, and he leaves. I look forward as she stands there still with an awkward gaze.

"Zaeden..." she starts awkwardly as she plays fingers. A smile threatens to leave my lips but I compose myself. " I know I'm wrong that I didn't text you or leave any message for you but I'm sorry I just...."

I know right now she's doubting herself and blaming herself for whatever happened but she can't blame herself. Without causing much complication between us, I turn toward her and look at her eyes, which used to be such a blazing eye in them.

She's tired, everything that has happened has also taken a toll on her, she was also away for one whole year from her family and friends. Why didn't I think of that? guilty reside in my body. Her gaze changes as she looks at my face. " Zaeden what happened?" she comes closer to my face and her warm rough palm reaches my cheeks.

Fuck those hands, I miss that hands. I close my eyes in her warmth as she rubs her palms on my cheeks lightly. "I missed you, Lily." The words left my mouth before I could think. I feel her body closer to mine before it could be.

"I missed you too." I look up to see tears in her eyes as she smiles brightly. Her eyes were already a bit puffy because she had already cried. But it doesn't concern me much it's the glow in her eyes that looks at me which makes me already want to devour her again.

My mouth stretches into a smile as she looks at me like that. Her lips also curl into smiles as she realizes that I'm not angry with her. "Are you not angry at me?" I smile more brightly than hers and answer her.

" I'm angry at you but maybe it is more selfish and childish. But I'm more happy that you're standing in front of me. " she smiles more as her tears fall on her cheeks. My hand wipes the lone tear from her face as she closes her eyes. "I'm sorry." the lone makes my heart sad but still I keep my control and try not to show her.

"You don't have to act in front of me. Scream at me, scold me, do anything but please don't ignore me don't ignore your feelings." Her hands come to me where my heart is present but my gaze is locked with hers.

Somehow it is intimidating as her sharp eyes are connected with someone who is as devil and cold yet she makes me want to love her all over again. The way she is nervously fiddling with her fingers, as she tries to put her weight on her one leg, the way she is biting her lip.

The way she is looking is making it hard for her. " I'm angry at you but it doesn't make sense that it was your fault. I understand that it was hectic to move from one place to another continuously and without having any friends or family on your back I do understand.

And don't think about whatever Sam says he's a brat. she laughs and that is what makes my day. "I think you've gotten to know him already. " she chuckles more as I reply. " Yeah, the whole year he was behind my ass. It was like carrying a big carriage on my back." And I know what she's thinking right now as she hides her red on the cheeks.

" And that's you isn't it? " She doesn't answer me and hides her face. My fingers find her chin as I hold it up to look at me. Her fluttering gaze finds mine and it locks and for a minute we are lost in each other and continue to stare at each other.

Our faces inch closer and the more I see her It's hard for me to stop loving her. "What are you doing? " Her voice booms out and a smile wants to leave my lips I stop them. "What do you think Lil cat? " I exclaim. The way her lips curl into the biggest smiles I have ever seen and the way her eyes shine bright. This is what I wanted to have, nothing but the shine in her eyes and the smiles.

The words which were trying to lose the shit leave my mouth as her eyes furrow in confusion. "We are going on a vacation." The smile on her lips suddenly vanishes and a frown can be seen on her.

"What? " My face counters in a 'didn't you hear me' look. "I mean I did hear you but a vacation suddenly." I sigh loudly and hold my hair in frustration.

" I know this is sudden and I have all things ready and It just came to my head and I thought you would need some- "

Before I could finish my sentence her hands came around my neck as she pulled me closer to her body and latched her lips with mine. Her lips move perfectly with mine as she slides her tongue inside my mouth. A few minutes later we pull out as her next words make my heart flutter.

" Wherever you take me Zaeden I'll be behind you because this time I won't be going anywhere ."

_____

30. Secluded Haven

Lily Rose

The forest cradled me, its ancient arms enfolding my secrets and scars. Zaeden led the way, our footsteps soft on the carpet of fallen leaves. Sunlight filtered through the canopy, dappling our faces, and I wondered what stories these trees whispered to one another.

"Why here?" I asked, my heart fluttering like a trapped bird.

"Because," Zaeden murmured, his voice a caress, "here, it's just us. No distractions, no prying eyes. Only the rustle of leaves and the memories etched into the bark."

We reached a small clearing—a moss-covered rock serving as our makeshift seat. Zaeden's touch lingered as he brushed my hair back. "Tell me about your year," he said, his eyes searching mine.

And so, under the watchful eyes of those ancient oaks, I spoke. Of distant lands, of sunsets over foreign seas. Zaeden listened, his gaze unwavering. He told me of sleepless nights, counting stars and wondering if I was doing the same.

As night fell, Zaeden built a fire. Its warm glow illuminated our faces, casting flickering shadows on the surrounding trees. We sat close, fingers entwined, and the crackling flames seemed to echo our shared longing.

"I love you," Zaeden whispered, his lips brushing against mine.

My heart swelled. "I love you too, Zaeden. Always."

And there, in the forest's heart, we found solace—a love unyielding, a promise whispered among the leaves. The stars above bore witness, and the wind carried our words to the farthest corners of the world.

But as Zaeden led me deeper into the forest, I realized I didn't know where we were headed. The trees closed in, their branches forming a protective canopy. The air grew cooler, and anticipation danced along my skin.

"Zaeden," I said, my voice barely audible. "Where are we going?"

He turned, his eyes alight with mischief. "Somewhere magical," he replied. "A place where time stands still."

And so we walked, hand in hand, deeper into the heart of the forest. The ground softened beneath our feet, and the world outside faded away. I trusted Zaeden—I had to. For in this secluded haven, destiny had brought us together, and perhaps, just perhaps, it would allow us to stay.

The forest enveloped us, its ancient trees leaning in as if conspirators in our love story. Zaeden's hand tightened around mine, and I followed him deeper, my heartbeat echoing the rhythm of our steps. The air grew cooler, and anticipation danced along my skin.

"Where are we going?" I asked again, my voice barely audible. But Zaeden only smiled, his eyes alight with secrets.

The path narrowed, and the trees leaned closer, their leaves brushing against my cheeks. I stumbled over a root, and Zaeden caught me effortlessly. His touch sent shivers down my spine—a promise of safety, of something more.

"Patience," he murmured, his lips brushing my forehead. "We're almost there."

And then, like a curtain parting, the forest revealed its hidden treasure. A wooden villa stood before us, nestled among the trees. Its walls were the colour of honey, and the windows sparkled like forgotten stars. Smoke curled from the chimney, and the scent of pine and warmth enveloped me.

"Zaeden," I breathed, my heart swelling. "Is this—?"

"Our sanctuary," he finished. "A place where time bends to our will."

He led me inside, and the villa unfolded—a cosy living room with a crackling fireplace, a kitchen where sunlight spilt through the window, and a bedroom with a bed draped in soft linens. The walls bore scars of love—carvings, initials, promises made in whispered darkness.

"How did you find this place?" I asked, my voice hushed.

"It found me," Zaeden replied. "Or perhaps destiny guided me here. Either way, it's ours now."

We explored every corner—the creaky wooden floors, the hidden nooks where secrets nestled. Zaeden had stocked the kitchen with fruits, wine, and chocolate—the essentials for a love-struck getaway. And outside, a wooden swing hung from a sturdy branch, inviting us to sway beneath the canopy.

"Lily," Zaeden said, pulling me close. *"This is where we'll write our story. Away from the world, away from time."

And so we did. We cooked together, our laughter mingling with the crackling fire. We danced in the moonlight, our shadows stretching across the wooden floor. We whispered secrets—of dreams, of fears, of forever.

"I missed you," I confessed one night, curled against Zaeden's chest. *"Every day."

"And I you," he replied, his fingers tracing patterns on my skin. "But now, we have this. Our haven."

Days blurred into nights, and the forest held us in its embrace. We made love under the stars, our breaths mingling with the rustle of leaves. Zaeden's kisses tasted of pine and promises, and I clung to him as if he were my lifeline.

"Come get up I'll show you something." he gets up and holds his hand for me to take. " Where are you taking me? How many surprises are there for you to show me." He shushed me and walked ahead. " Terrace." One word what he had spilt.

The night air clung to my skin as Zaeden led me up the narrow staircase to the terrace. The city sprawled below, a tapestry of twinkling lights. I followed him, my heart fluttering with anticipation. What surprise awaited me?

The hot tub sat there, its water shimmering under the moon's watchful gaze. Zaeden gestured for me to climb in, and I hesitated for a moment before lowering myself into the warm embrace of the bubbles. The tension in my shoulders eased as the heat enveloped me.

he came closer to me and removed my shirt slowly and threw it somewhere-I didn't know because I was captivated by his eyes, he didn't remove his eyes away from me as he removed my shirt, my pants, and the rubber tie from my hair to let my hair fall.

slowly his hands glided my hand to his waistband of pants. My hands removed his pants without breaking the eye contact. It was intimate when I slowly removed his pants and threw them out. His hands came around my waist as he pulled me toward him.

I bit my lip in excitement as Zaeden's lips curved into a smirk as he said. " Why are you smiling Lil Cat? " I shrugged my shoulders. " I don't know. " His lips grazed mine as he slowly whispered.

"Is it you don't know? " I looked into his eyes brought my lips more closer to his and replied.

" Maybe you know why I am smiling, Mr.Carter. " He smiled before colliding his lips with mine. The kiss was different from others, he wasn't holding me like he usually did, and he didn't kiss me like he owned me- he kissed me like he loved me. A smile broke on my lips as we kissed.

"Zaeden," I said, my voice barely above a whisper, "why are we here?"

He settled across from me, his eyes holding mine. "Because," he replied, "sometimes healing begins in unexpected places." We talked—about life, dreams, and the constellations above. His laughter was infectious, and for a while, I forgot about the stalker who haunted my every step. The night embraced us, cocooning us in its quiet magic.

As the clock neared midnight, Zaeden stood up, his silhouette outlined against the cityscape. He disappeared briefly, and when he returned, he held a handful of paper lanterns. Their colours danced in the breeze, and he released them one by one into the night sky.

"Happy birthday, Lily," he said softly, his voice carrying a weight I couldn't comprehend. My mind raced. My birthday? I hadn't celebrated it in years. Not since that fateful day—the day my father had forced me to do the unthinkable.

Maria, my mother, had been my refuge. Her love had shielded me from my father's wrath, but on that day, he'd demanded loyalty in blood. I'd killed her to survive, to prove my allegiance to his twisted empire. The memory was a blur, a nightmare I'd buried deep within.

Zaeden's smile faded as he noticed my hesitation. "Lily, what's wrong?"

I swallowed the lump in my throat. "I don't celebrate my birthday," I whispered. "Today was the anniversary of Maria's death. Sixteen years ago, I became a killer."

His eyes widened, and he reached for my hand. "You've carried that burden alone for too long," he said. "Let me share it with you."

And so, as the lanterns floated higher, I let Zaeden hold me. Maybe this birthday would be different—a step toward healing, toward reclaiming my life from the shadows. His warmth enveloped me, and for the first time, I dared to believe that love could mend even the deepest wounds.

"But his words warmed me," I continued, my voice barely audible. "So from today, let's celebrate it—for a fresh start."

Zaeden's gaze softened, and he pulled me closer. "Together," he murmured as if promising to rewrite the painful chapters of my past. The lanterns painted the sky with hope, and I allowed myself to believe that maybe, just maybe, this birthday could mark the beginning of something beautiful.

We stayed in the hot tub until the lanterns faded into the horizon. Zaeden's arms held me, and I realized that healing wasn't a solitary journey. Perhaps, with him by my side, I could find solace in the night, in the warmth of his touch, and the promise of a fresh start.

The lanterns floated higher, their glow fading into the vastness of the night. Zaeden's arms held me, and I leaned into his warmth. The hot tub's water cradled us, cocooning our secrets and scars.

And so, as the clock struck midnight, I whispered, "Thank you, Zaeden."

He kissed my forehead. "Happy birthday, Lily."

And in that quiet moment, as the clock struck midnight, I allowed myself to believe that maybe—just maybe—this night could be more than a painful reminder. Maybe it was the beginning of something beautiful—a fresh start under the moonlight.

We stayed on the terrace, wrapped in each other's presence. The city hummed below, oblivious to our fragile hearts. Zaeden's fingers traced patterns on my arm, and I closed my eyes, savouring the warmth seeping into my bones.

"Tell me about Maria," he said softly. "About your mother."

I hesitated, the memories rising like ghosts. "She loved roses," I began. "Their delicate petals, the way they bloomed even in adversity. She used to say they held secrets—the kind that whispered hope."

Zaeden listened, his gaze unwavering. I told him about Maria's laughter, her hands kneading dough for fresh bread, the lullabies she sang when I couldn't sleep. And then I told him about that final night—the night my father's rage had shattered our haven.

"She shielded me," I said, my voice trembling. "Told me to run, to survive. And I did what I had to."

Zaeden's thumb brushed away a tear. "Survival isn't a sin," he murmured. "But you've carried this burden alone for too long."

I leaned into him, seeking solace. "Why now, Zaeden? Why this birthday?"

His eyes held mine, their depths unfathomable. "Because sometimes healing begins in unexpected places," he echoed his earlier words. "And because you deserve more than shadows."

We sat there, two broken souls seeking redemption. The moon watched over us, its silver glow illuminating our scars. And as the night deepened, Zaeden whispered promises—promises of shared burdens, of fresh starts, of love that could mend even the deepest wounds.

And so, beneath the moon's gaze, I allowed myself to believe.

For the first time in years, I allowed myself to believe that birthdays could be more than painful reminders—they could be a chance to rewrite our stories, to find love amidst the scars.

"Will it last?" I asked, watching the night paint the sky.

"As long as we want it to," Zaeden said. "Time bends here, remember? We can make eternity in a heartbeat."

And so we did. We carved our initials into the villa's walls, a testament to our love. We whispered vows among the trees, and the wind carried them to the farthest corners of the world.

"Always," Zaeden promised, his lips against mine. "Forever."

And there, in our secluded haven, destiny surrendered. Zaeden and I wove our love into the very fabric of the forest, and time stood still—for us, for our whispered promises, for our forever.

———————

Lily's night unfolds, and Zaeden becomes her beacon of hope.

31. Darkness[1]

Zaeden Carter

The night we were wrapped around us like a velvet cloak. Lily lay beside me on the terrace couch, her skin warm against mine. The duvet cocooned us, its softness a barrier against the chill. Above, the stars sparkled, indifferent to our fragile existence.

Lily's breathing was steady, her lashes casting delicate shadows on her cheeks. I traced the curve of her jaw, marvelling at the resilience etched there. She'd survived horrors I couldn't fathom, yet her spirit remained unbroken.

The lanterns we'd released earlier had vanished into the vastness, their colours fading like forgotten dreams. But here, with Lily beside me, hope rekindled. Maybe we could rewrite our stories, and stitch together the frayed edges of our souls.

I shifted closer, my arm slipping beneath the duvet to pull her against my chest. Her hair smelled of rain and secrets. "Lily," I whispered, "you're not alone anymore."

She stirred, her eyes fluttering open. Moonlight painted her features—vulnerable, yet fierce. "Zaeden," she murmured, "why now? Why this kindness?"

I brushed my thumb across her lips. "Because sometimes, even broken things deserve tenderness."

Her gaze held mine, and for a moment, we were suspended—two lost souls seeking solace in the night. "What happens next?" she asked.

I leaned down, my lips grazing hers. "Next," I whispered, "we heal. Together."

And so, beneath the star-studded sky, we slept—naked, vulnerable, and entwined. The city's distant hum faded, replaced by the rhythm of our shared breaths. Maybe love could bloom here, like those roses Maria had cherished—the kind that whispered hope.

As dawn approached, I vowed to protect Lily from the darkness. We'd face our demons, chase away the shadows, and create a new story—one where birthdays held promise, and scars became constellations.

The sun peeked through the terrace railing, casting a warm glow on Lily's sleeping form. Her lashes fluttered, and I wondered what dreams danced behind her closed eyes. The duvet had slipped, revealing the curve of her shoulder, and the delicate arch of her neck.

I shifted, careful not to wake her. The night had been a revelation—a tapestry of vulnerability and shared secrets. I'd held her, kissed her, whispered promises against her skin. And now, as dawn painted the sky, I vowed to protect this fragile connection.

Lily stirred, her lips curving into a half-smile. "Zaeden," she murmured, "you're staring."

I chuckled. "Guilty as charged."

She sat up, rubbing her eyes. "What's the plan for today?"

I leaned closer, my lips grazing her temple. "Breakfast first. Then... adventures."

We sat on the terrace, sipping coffee and sharing stories. Lily's laughter was like sunlight breaking through storm clouds. She told me about her childhood, the games she'd played with Maria, the stolen moments of joy amidst the chaos.

I listened, my heart aching. "You're stronger than you know," I said. "Surviving doesn't make you a killer."

She looked at me, vulnerability in her eyes. "And you? What's your story, Zaeden?"

I hesitated, the memories resurfacing like ghosts. "My parents," I began, "they were everything. We lived in a small house near the woods, where the air smelled of pine and adventure. My father taught me to play the guitar, and my mother—she had this laugh that could light up the darkest room."

Lily leaned closer. "What happened?"

I looked away, tracing the rim of my coffee cup. "One night, they didn't come home. A car accident. I was fourteen." The pain still lingered, a dull ache in my chest.

"And Chris?" Lily prompted.

"Chris was my neighbour," I continued. "His parents took me in. They were kind, but their house felt foreign—too neat, too quiet. Chris and I became brothers, bound by loss. We'd sneak out at night, explore the woods, and dream of escaping."

Lily's fingers brushed mine. "And your music?"

"It was my lifeline," I confessed. "I'd sit by the window, strumming my guitar, hoping my parents would hear. Music became my way to connect with them, to keep their memory alive."

She smiled. "You're still connected, Zaeden. Through your songs."

I nodded, grateful for her understanding. "Maybe," I said, "this fresh start is my chance to honour them—to find light amidst the shadows."

I hesitated, then told her about my past—the glass towers, the corporate wars, the emptiness that had driven me to the edge. "I've done things," I admitted. "Things I regret."

Lily reached for my hand. "We all have shadows," she said. "But maybe we can find light together."

The shower was small, but Lily fit perfectly against my chest. Steam enveloped us, blurring the lines between skin and soul. She traced the scars on my back, her gentle and demanding touch.

"Why did you save me?" she asked, her voice echoing off the tiles.

I kissed her forehead. "Because you're worth saving."

She laughed, the sound echoing through the bathroom. "Mischievous Zaeden," she teased. "Always with the hero complex."

I pulled her closer, our bodies moulding together. "Maybe I just want to be your hero."

We dressed, the morning air cool against our skin. Lily led me to the corner of the terrace where a makeshift shooting range awaited. Bulls-eye targets hung from strings, swaying in the breeze.

"Gun games?" I raised an eyebrow.

She grinned, handing me a toy gun. "Trust me."

We stood side by side, the sun warming our backs. Lily's eyes locked on mine, determination in their depths. She raised her gun, aimed, and fired. The dart hit dead centre.

I blinked. "Impressive."

She winked. "Your turn."

I aimed, but my gaze remained on her. "Lily," I said, "you're my bulls-eye."

And as I shot, hitting the mark, I realized that maybe—just maybe—this mischievous, broken girl could be my salvation.

We spent the day exploring, laughing, stealing kisses in hidden corners. The city blurred around us, its noise fading into insignificance. Lily's hand fit perfectly in mine, her laughter like a melody.

As the sun dipped below the horizon, we returned to the terrace. The lanterns had vanished, but Lily's eyes held their glow. "Thank you," she whispered.

I kissed her, tasting hope and redemption. I said. "Let's begin again."

And so, beneath the fading light, we did.

The forest enveloped us, its ancient secrets woven into every rustling leaf. Lily's laughter echoed through the trees, and I watched her twirl, her hair catching the sunlight. We were like children, lost in a world of green and possibility.

"Zaeden," she called, her eyes bright, "can you feel it?"

I nodded, my senses alive. The wind whispered secrets—the stories of every branch, every blade of grass. "It's like the forest is singing," I said. "A symphony of life."

She danced closer, her hand brushing mine. "And we're part of it," she murmured. "Tiny notes in this grand composition."

We wandered deeper, the ground soft beneath our feet. The trees leaned in, their leaves brushing against our skin. "Tell me," Lily said, "what's your favourite sound in the forest?"

I closed my eyes, listening. "The creaking of branches," I replied. "It's like the trees are talking to each other, sharing their secrets."

She laughed. "And what do they say?"

I hesitated, then confessed, "They say that love is like the wind—unseen but always felt."

Lily's fingers traced patterns on my chest. "And what else?"

I leaned closer, my lips brushing her ear. "They say," I whispered, "that sometimes, even broken things can find solace in each other."

We found a clearing, the sun casting dappled shadows on the forest floor. Lily's eyes sparkled with mischief. "Let's play," she said.

"Play what?" I asked, intrigued.

She grinned. "Deadly games."

I raised an eyebrow. "Deadly?"

She pointed to the wind, lifting strands of her hair. "See that breeze? It's our opponent."

I chuckled. "And how do we play?"

"We challenge the wind," she explained. "We race it, dance with it, become one with it."

I watched as she spun, her dress billowing. "And what's the prize?"

She leaned close, her lips brushing mine. "The thrill," she whispered. "The feeling of being alive."

And so, we played—chasing the wind, laughing as it eluded us. We became children again, carefree and wild. The forest watched, its ancient heart beating in rhythm with ours.

Lily Rose

I felt a heavy gaze on my back as I turned around to see Zaeden staring at my dress. A chuckle left my lips as his eyes continued to stare at my dress. "What are you staring at Zaeden? "   " Is that a new dress? " He asked ignoring my question.

I smiled before answering him. " It is. Isn't it beautiful? " I asked looking at my dress. His answer came. " Indeed it is. " I smiled. " It is- ." His voice cut out before I could say something. "Remove them. " His voice was sharp, rough, hoarse and deep filled with desire.

My eyes met his, his brown orbs were now dark- filled with lust. A rush of adrenaline and coldness rushed my spine. His steps were adamant about my refusals. I knew I was stuck in this forest and I couldn't run.

My hands reached my back zip down the dress. The dress fell as he stopped in front of me. I trusted him, I knew way better than to run away from him. His hands rounded my waist pulling me closer as his lips crashed down mine.

How the hell does his lips taste so fucking good. His lips tasted better and better the more I kissed him. I couldn't get enough of his lips, of his taste, of him. It was becoming a big problem, and it was something I needed to resolve soon.

Zaeden groaned into the kiss and his hand was in my hair within a moment. Bringing me closer wasn't enough for him, from what I could tell. He pulled us down and had me on his lap quickly. I felt his hard-on over the clothes and I was already struggling to suppress the desire to fuck him in this forest.

"Zaeden, wait," I managed to mumble and slightly make a gap between us, "Someone will see us." His response was a mere chuckle. "So what? Don't tell me you're getting shy now." He teased me and placed another kiss, though it was on my jaw, and he slowly made his way down my neck.

My head flew back and I bit my bottom lip to prevent moans from slipping. He paused and leaned back slowly, eyes darkened and eyes narrowed. Something between an animalistic growl and a hiss slipped past his mouth, "Let them see."

His hands were under my clothes quickly. His cold hands on my hot skin made me ache, and burn with desire. The moment he cupped my breasts underneath the bra I was moaning, gone, and definitely in need of a good fuck.

Zaeden was getting more aroused as the time passed, too. I could feel the growth down there, and the sudden twitching from time to time. I saw his cock through the zipper, and him being fully clothed, it was one of the hottest sights in my life.

I hissed lowly as he lowered me onto himself, halfway through slowly. He paused for a moment before he gripped my hips tightly and slammed me down onto his cock in one motion. I felt full, overwhelmed and excited.

"That's it," Zaeden said, "You're taking me so well, Lil Cat " It was more of a whisper and it made my whole skin ache. It was likely the need to have his lips all over my skin, to be covered in his kisses. I was beginning to feel overwhelmed.

It wasn't just the sex, it was that somehow, this particular position was awakening something deeply inside of me. Perhaps I was delusional, perhaps even crazy, but my heart ached. It felt so good yet too sad.

It didn't quite hit me yet how much I'd allowed myself to truly feel. As quickly as I was getting attached to people, it went just as slow to completely detach myself from them. And Zaeden? As dumb as it sounded, in my heart, he was one of a kind.

A person different from anyone I'd met in my years, and the stoic, cold and bored expressions he would usually treat me with were the reason I felt the attraction in the first place. I knew myself well enough before I started this bullshit.

Why the fuck did it seem like a good idea to try and get with a man who was not only almost twice my age but also emotionally unavailable? There was no point in doing this and I wanted to cry. As if he noticed the shift in my mood, he picked up the pace.

Slow kisses were placed all over my neck and collarbone until his lips landed on mine. In a cry, I released all the built-up anger and sadness into an orgasm that seemed to never end. Zaeden followed suit.

With a low groan, he placed his head on my shoulder as he exploded inside of me. He laid like that for a while, whilst we regained our composure. Sex in the forest was something I couldn't explain. Something magical, deadly, and simple yet filled with joys and moans.

As evening approached, we found a rocky outcrop. The sun dipped low, painting the sky in hues of gold and crimson. Zaeden nestled against me, his head on my shoulder.

"Look," I said, pointing westward. "The sunset."

He held his breath. The mountains stood sentinel, their peaks aflame. The forest whispered its approval, and I hummed a tune—a melody as old as time.

"Sing with me," I urged.

And so, as the sun sank below the horizon, we sang—a duet of wind and heartbeats. The forest joined in, its leaves rustling in harmony. For that fleeting moment, we were part of something greater—a symphony of love and longing.

As darkness settled, Zaeden kissed me, his lips tasting of sunsets and promises. "Tomorrow," he said, "we'll play again."

And I knew—whether deadly games or whispered serenades—the forest held magic, and Zaeden was my muse.

———————————

Zaeden's past echoes, and Lily becomes his confidante.

32. Redemption

L ily Rose

The forest had released us and spat us out onto the edge of civilization. Zaeden and I emerged, dishevelled and weary, from the dense canopy. The sun hung low, casting elongated shadows across the path that led back to Chris's house—the mansion that held secrets as ancient as the gnarled oaks we'd left behind.

But before we could cross the threshold, Chris's mother, Eleanor, materialized like a vengeful spirit. Her eyes bore into Zaeden, and her voice sliced through the air. "You've taken her away,"

The air crackled with tension as we stepped into Chris's house. The familiar scent of polished wood and old memories enveloped me, and I fought to steady my breath. Chaos erupted—the kind that swirls around old wounds and buried secrets. Chris's mother, Mrs Aiden, charged at Zaeden like a hurricane. Her fury was palpable, fueled by years of resentment.

As we approached, the grandeur of the estate loomed before us. The wrought-iron gates creaked open, and the gravel crunched under our shoes. The mansion stood like a sentinel, its stone facade both welcoming and foreboding. I glanced at Zaeden, wondering how he felt about stepping into this web of intrigue.

"You!" she spat, her voice a serrated blade. "You took her away!"

Zaeden staggered back, absorbing the blows. The room watched—the aunts, the cousins, even the nosy neighbour from next door. They laughed, their joy echoing off the walls. To them, it was a spectacle—a family drama they could savour over dinner.

We entered the grand hallway, where laughter echoed off the marble walls. Chris's father, Sam, and other guests mingled, oblivious to the storm brewing. For a moment, I allowed myself to believe that maybe—just maybe—life could be simple again.

And for me, it was a relief. Relief that the spotlight had shifted, that my escape had gone unnoticed. I clung to the fringes, my heart racing. Before Eleanor could retort, the mansion doors swung open. Chris appeared, his eyes wide with shock. "Lily?" he whispered, his voice cracking. "You're back." I embraced him, feeling the tremors in his frame.

I smiled. " Of course, I wouldn't leave you guys alone, you're my best buddy." He smiled before hugging me once more. " We have a lot of things to discuss, and there's a tea to spill too." He exclaimed loudly and a burst of laughter echoed.

"Sam," I murmured. My voice was low, more in a whisper. After our heartbreaking meeting, he still had a pleasant for me. His eyes shone bright which had told me he was out of his nightmares.

"Li." He came around my waist pulling my face closer to his chest. "it's time for change. The legacy—the papers—they're mine no longer."

But then, Ken—the ever-efficient secretary—strode in, his expression unreadable.

"Lily," he said, his tone clipped, "we need your signature."

My breath hitched. The papers were there—cold and official. They spelt out my fate—then the transfer of responsibilities, the end of my days as a protector. Sam, my brother, would take the reins. I'd saved him countless times, put his needs above mine. But now, it was over.

The weight of the world settled on my shoulders. The papers—my father's pact with darkness—had kept our family in power for generations. But it had come at a cost: the lives of innocent women and children. I had been their saviour, their protector. But now, it was time to pass the torch.

Zaeden's anger flared. "Move out," he growled at Ken. "Get out of here."

Ken remained stoic. "I'm just doing my job," he said. "Lily, sign them." Ken's voice boomed. He knew what was happening, the time was ticking, and I was rethinking about the decisions.

Sam had finally wanted to take responsibility for the legacy in this dangerous world, the brother who I had always thought of putting before me now wanted to do something for me. A sacrifice Is what I have always done. Maria was my first and the second was leaving my brother with my father's dark tempt.

"Lily, sign those papers. What are you thinking? This is for the best, for you, for Sam, for us. Blue Knight is now going to be passed to Sam and I'm sure he won't let you down."

I looked at the papers—the ink lines that severed my ties. My illusions shattered—the belief that I could save everyone, that love conquered all. But sometimes, love was a double-edged sword—a choice between self-preservation and sacrifice.

I took the pen, my hand trembling. "Sam," I whispered, "Thank you for doing this for me."

The papers lay on the antique desk—the inkwell waiting. As I picked up the pen, I wondered if redemption was possible. If breaking free from my father's legacy would finally grant me peace.

And so, in the dimly lit study, I signed my name. The ink flowed, sealing my fate and unravelling the threads of a twisted past. As the mansion walls absorbed our whispered promises, I vowed to protect, heal, and rewrite our story—one choice at a time.

And as I signed my name, I knew—the days of saving my brother were over. It was time to save myself and begin a new life for me, Zaeden and Sam.

Outside, laughter echoed—the guests oblivious to the seismic shift within these walls. But for me, the weight lifted. The papers lay signed, their ink drying. Sam would lead, and I would find my path—one that didn't demand sacrifice.

My mood had drifted suddenly I felt light but guilty, guilty for putting my brother's life into this. A hand came around my shoulders. I looked up to find Sam's bright eyes on me. His lips lift into a smile.

A small smile is what I could offer him. " Come on spend this day with me. Let's watch some movie, and have some of your favourite cheese popcorn with a shot of tequila." A chuckle left my lips. " You still remember that ?" His smile lifts more broadly. " Of course How can I forget that Li that was such a hilarious moment of all. " A big smile is now what I could offer him.

I lifted my lips to his ear to whisper. " And you loved it. " he smiled. " That's obvious because that was the first you made me drink alcohol and that was the day when I was first ever drunk." A chuckle left my lips as memories filled my mind.

I couldn't see the anxious Lily killing her mother but I could see myself laughing and sneaking some snacks into Sam's room. Our rooms were away from each other where we couldn't pass by yet we still loved each other and you knew better than others what our eyes could hold at night, and our better versions could seen by us only.

But now I was free from protecting my brother and sacrificing more lives, Sam knows what Blue Knight brings him into but still, for me, he fought his battles and now what I could offer him was support.

Support is what I could give him without letting his demons stalk him. I looked at him and smiled brightly, his eyes shone brightly and he knew the smile I was offering him was real.   " Thanks for doing this Sam, I would never be able to thank you off properly," I said.

"Li what you've done is not even compared to what I'm doing. You've been away for most of your life to what, save the people, save me but what about you? Go on Li spend your remaining time creating memories, joys and what shit you missed. I love you and I always will."

A tear left my eye at his words. "You've grown up a lot Sam and I'm proud of you, I always will." He smiled and I knew at that moment I was free and my brother wasn't afraid to take my legacy, my name- Blue Knight.

"I'll get back with you in the room with popcorn and tequila hmm? " I nodded at his words as he walked out with Ken. Zaeden was beside me as he kissed my forehead.

As we left the study, Zaeden's hand in mine, I glanced at the portrait of my father. His eyes followed me, accusing and hollow. But I no longer bore his sins. The legacy was no longer mine alone.

In the grand hallway, I paused. "Zaeden," I said, "what now?"

He smiled—a rare, genuine smile. "Now," he said, "we live."

We continued, hand in hand, our footsteps leaving imprints on the earth. The uncertain future stretched before us, but I knew one thing: I would protect, rewrite, and love fiercely. The ruins held promise—the promise of something new.

And so we stepped into the uncertain future, leaving behind the ghosts of our past. The mansion doors closed, and the sun dipped below the horizon. But within me, a spark ignited—a promise to protect, to rewrite, and to find love amidst the ruins.

And so, beneath the moon's watchful eye, we walked—a saviour and her ally—into the night, ready to create our destiny.

––––––––––

Lily and Zaeden's journey—fraught with secrets, sacrifice, and love—left indelible marks on the mansion's walls. As they stepped into the uncertain future, they carried with them the echoes of laughter, the weight of responsibility, and the promise of redemption. Their story became a testament to rewriting one's fate, finding solace amidst ruins, and embracing love as the ultimate act of defiance.

33. Rewrite

Lily Rose

The night unfolded like a secret—the kind that whispered promises and held the weight of memories. Sam and I sat cross-legged on the plush living room carpet, surrounded by a fortress of pillows. The flickering screen cast shadows on the walls, and the scent of buttered popcorn hung in the air.

The movie playing in the background brought nostalgia. "Li, do you remember us sneaking out on the treehouse just to watch the little shows? " I smiled nodding my head. " Of course Sam Every Tuesday night we would sneak out. " He hummed.

" Those days were not good, those created demons for us but in those moments we still shared our little moments which helped our demons to stay away." Sam sighed as he rested his head on my shoulder.

"Sam," I said, my voice conspiratorial, "this is our rebellion."

He grinned, his eyes alight. "Rebellion against what, Lily?"

"Against the legacy," I replied. "Against the darkness that once consumed us."

The movie played—a classic, something about star-crossed lovers. But it didn't matter. The real magic was in the room—the laughter that bubbled up, the clink of tequila glasses, and the way Sam snorted when the hero made a grand declaration.

And then, as if summoned by our joy, Chris appeared. His silhouette framed the doorway, and I forgot to breathe for a moment. He wore a faded T-shirt, his hair tousled. The years had been kind to him—etched character into his features.

"Am I interrupting?" Chris asked, his voice soft.

"No," Sam said, patting the empty spot beside him. "Join us."

Chris settled in, and suddenly, the room felt smaller and cosier. The movie played on, but our attention shifted—to shared glances, to memories that danced just beyond reach.

"A year passed but I still remember how Zaeden got jealous once and Oh, the day was nothing but torture to him. I mean at the end of the day Lily got fucke- Ouchh! " Chris screamed as I hit him playfully on the head.

"Remember when we used to sneak into the kitchen at night?" Chris said, his eyes crinkling. "Popcorn and tequila—our secret recipe." Chris laughed as if reminiscing about the memory.   "Excuse me that's my recipe I was the one who made that thing. "

Sam raised his glass. "To rebellion," he said.

"To rewrite our story," I added, and we clinked our glasses.

The movie faded into background noise. We talked—about everything and nothing. About the mansion, the legacy, and the women we'd saved. About love lost and found.

Chris nudged me. "You left," he said, "but you came back."

"I had to," I replied. "To break free."

Sam leaned back, his gaze on the ceiling. "And Zaeden?"

I hesitated. "He's my ally," I said. "My confidant."

Chris chuckled. "Sounds serious."

"It is," I admitted. "But love doesn't absolve us of responsibility."

And so, in that dimly lit room, we laughed until tears blurred our vision. The movie ended, but our night continued—a tapestry of shared history, forgiveness and redemption.

The night wrapped around us like a velvet cloak. Our steps echoed until we were on the balcony. The balcony cradled our secrets—the wooden floor cool against our skin. Chris, Sam, and I sat in a triangle of vulnerability, the moon our silent witness.

The stars danced, their choreography ancient and unyielding. I traced constellations with my finger, connecting dots that held stories—of gods, heroes, and lost lovers. Sam leaned back, his laughter echoing from the depths of his soul. Chris, ever enigmatic, stared into the abyss beyond the railing.

"Remember," Sam said, his voice a whiskey-soaked melody, "when we were kids? We'd sneak out here, wrapped in blankets, pretending the night was our canvas."

Chris smirked. "And you'd recite terrible poetry."

Sam raised an eyebrow. "Terrible? My haikus were masterpieces."

I leaned into the bannister, the wood rough against my cheek. "What about you, Chris? Any hidden talents?"

He glanced at me, his eyes unreadable. "I can juggle," he deadpanned. "Three rubber ducks."

Sam snorted. "Rubber ducks again? Is that your legacy?"

Chris's gaze softened. "Maybe," he said. "They float, you know? Unsinkable."

The moon hung low, its silver path stretching across the ocean. I wondered if it whispered secrets to the tides—of lost ships, forgotten promises, and love that defied time.

"Zaeden," I said, "where is he now?"

"He's out there," Chris replied. "Watching over us." I shook my head. "I don't know the moment he's had enough of us I'm done and might my legs be. " Both of them laughed as their laughter brought smiles to my face.

Sam nudged me. "And you, Lily? What do you want?"

I closed my eyes, feeling the night seep into my bones. "Redemption," I said. "A chance to rewrite the story by the hands of my own."

Chris leaned on the railing, his silhouette sharp against the moonlight. "We're all broken," he said. " We are all broken, damaged, used and ruined but that doesn't mean we aren't given any chance to live life. " I said my words which in despair created a meaning for us.

"But maybe broken things can still reflect light." Chris's voice came to life.

And so we sat—saviour, brother, and enigma—our laughter a fragile bridge across the chasm of our past. The night held its breath, waiting for our next move.

"Tomorrow," I whispered, "we face the truth."

Sam clinked his glass against mine. "To rewriting," he said.

"To love," Chris added, surprising us all.

"To legacy which my sister sacrificed her life and now I'll repay her," Sam said clinking the glasses.

And as the stars wove their tapestry above, we leaned into the night, ready to unravel secrets, find redemption, and maybe—just maybe—float like unsinkable rubber ducks.

As dawn approached, we sat on the balcony, watching the first light kiss the treetops. The legacy loomed behind us, but for now, we were free. The tequila bottle stood empty, and our laughter echoed into the morning.

And so, as the sun rose, we stepped into the uncertain future—the saviour, the brother, and the enigmatic man who had become something more. Our laughter lingered, a promise etched in the dawn.

The sun had fully risen, casting a warm glow on the balcony. Chris leaned against the railing, his expression a mix of mischief and gravity. "All right," he said, "you asked for it. Prepare yourselves for the juiciest tea I've been steeping in."

Sam and I exchanged amused glances. "Hit us," I said, settling cross-legged on the floor.

Chris cleared his throat, adopting a dramatic tone. "First off," he began, "Remember Mrs Abernathy, the ancient neighbour who always peeked through her curtains?"

I nodded. "The one who claimed her cat was a reincarnated poet?"

"That's the one," Chris confirmed. "Well, she swears she saw your father levitating in the garden once. Said he was communing with the spirits."

Sam snorted. "Levitating? Seriously?"

Chris shrugged. "Hey, it's tea, not truth serum."

I leaned closer. "More, Chris. Spill it."

"Okay," Chris said, leaning in. "My father's secret room? Turns out it wasn't just for records. He had a collection of—wait for it—antique rubber ducks."

I burst out laughing. "Rubber ducks?"

"Yep," Chris said. "He'd sit there, stroking their heads, muttering about world domination. I think the ducks were his advisors."

Sam wiped tears from his eyes. "This is gold."

"But wait," Chris said, lowering his voice. "The darkest secret? father's favourite bedtime story for you was—brace yourselves—' The Adventures of Sir Quackers and the Magical Bath.'"

Sam choked. "Sir Quackers?"

"Magical bath?" I added.

Chris nodded solemnly. "Legend has it that Sir Quackers defeated evil soap scum and brought peace to the porcelain kingdom."

We dissolved into laughter, the absurdity of it all echoing off the mansion walls.

"But," Chris said, his tone serious now, "there's one more thing. My father believed in a prophecy—a cryptic verse he'd recite during thunderstorms."

Sam leaned forward. "What prophecy?"

Chris leaned in, his eyes wide. "It went like this: 'When the moon wears a top hat, and the stars dance the cha-cha, the chosen one shall find the golden toilet brush.'"

Silence hung in the air. Then Sam burst out laughing. "The golden toilet brush? Seriously?"

Chris grinned. "I told you—the tea is wild."

As the morning wore on, we shared more stories—the mundane and the fantastical. The legacy seemed less oppressive now, more like a quirky family saga.

And so, as the sun climbed higher, we sat—saviour, brother, and friend—our laughter a balm for old wounds. The secrets split, and with each revelation, we rewrote our history. The golden toilet brush might be nonsense, but our bond was real.

The sun hung bright, its golden glow casting shadows on the balcony. Chris and Sam's laughter had faded into the night, leaving me alone with my thoughts. The sea whispered secrets, and I wondered if redemption was possible—if love could rewrite the jagged edges of our past.

And then, like a tempest, Zaeden appeared. His eyes blazed, and his hair tousled from the wind. He crossed the threshold, and before I could react, he took me in his arms.

"You had her for the whole night," Zaeden said, his voice a low growl. "Let me have her now." Before Sam and Chris could say anything he lifted me off.

His lips crashed against mine, and the world tilted. The balcony railing pressed into my back, but I didn't care. Zaeden tasted of salt and longing—a storm waiting to break.

"Guys get a room for yourselves." Chris's voice boomed as Sam laughed and the heat landed on my cheeks but Zaeden didn't pay a shit to them.

"Zaeden," I gasped, pulling away. "What—"

He silenced me with another kiss, his hands urgent on my waist. "I've waited," he murmured, "Watched you dance with ghosts and these damn stupid guys. But now, Lily, you're mine."

His possessiveness should have scared me, but it ignited something deeper—a hunger for connection, for rewriting our fractured story.

"Zaeden," I whispered, "I—"

He kissed me again, his mouth claiming mine. The moon bore witness as we unravelled—two broken souls seeking solace in each other. The legacy, the secrets—they blurred into insignificance.

"Redemption," Zaeden said against my lips, "is in your eyes."

And so, on that moonlit balcony, we wove our prophecy—a tale of love, defiance, and the promise of unsinkable hearts.

He lifted me and carried me towards the room his lips still descended on mine as he walked and barged into a room.

The morning bloomed, and Zaeden's patience wore thin. He barged in, his eyes ablaze, having had enough of the tantrums between Sam and Chris. But that's a story for another dawn. I knew this was never-ending for us.

He put me down and looked at me. He pulled me into a kiss. I kissed him back as if I was kissing him for the first time. I kissed him back trying to the pain from him and bring it to me. I kissed him, and I had no intention of stopping for the rest of my life.

My hand removed his shirt leaving him bare and naked to my eyes and I would devour him just like he always did.

"Let me take your pain away" I whispered against his lips running my hands over his bare chest and his skin bristled under my touch "Let me help you forget even for a while"

His tongue slips between my lips, deepening the kiss, and giving me the answer I needed. The warmth of his tongue against mine sends shivers directly down my spine. I can't stop and I won't stop.

I will do anything to take his pain away and make his mind at ease even for a while. Anything. Without taking my eyes off of him I slid down, kneeling in front of him. His hands gripped the table tightly around his fingers, looking down at me, clenching his jaw painfully as I unbuckled his belt. I know he needs me.

"Lily, don't do something you won't be able to end. " his voice was low and indecisive, but he still didn't stop me as I took off his pants, along with his boxers, freeing his already hard cock.

I wrapped my small hand around the base of his dick, running my tongue along its entire length without taking my eyes off of him. His features tightened beneath his black hair that fell in front.

"I love how easily I can turn you on" I murmured, swirling my tongue around his head and he just groaned in response, closing his eyes, and tilting his head back to give a perfect view of his neck. I have him completely at my mercy.

I took him all in my mouth, feeling him hit the back of my throat, making me choke but I loved it. I bobbed my head up and down along his length and Zaeden let me do as I pleased with him. He didn't push himself forward in my mouth or grab my hair roughly like he usually does. His hands still gripped the edge of the table, only groaning and taking everything I offered him.

His eyes watching me, consuming me and I'm sure he can hear how wet I am when I press my thighs together still using my mouth to please him.

"You're so beautiful from this angle, you know?" I whispered in an innocent voice, wrapping my tongue around his head like a lollipop, and he groaned again, licking his lips in response."Lily" he growled, his voice deep and low enough to make me moan with his dick deep in my mouth.

I tortured him with my mouth a little more, wanting to erase everything bad from his mind, and judging by his face I succeeded, because he was lost in his pleasure and his eyes were relaxed and watching his cock disappear between my lips.

When I decided enough was enough, I released his cock from my mouth with a bop, rising to my feet without taking my eyes off of him. I kissed him with an open mouth, sliding my tongue in his mouth, letting him himself, and he cupped my face in his hands, squeezing me closer, begging for more.

We kissed as his cock rubbed against my stomach covered only in his shirt I was wearing. Without breaking the kiss, I pulled him to the couch, pushing his body on it.

My mouth was watering as I watched his powerful figure sprawled on the couch with his messy wet hair, dark eyes, his hands leaning back, and his lap inviting me to join him.

He gave me a small sly smile as I removed the only other thing I had on my body, my thong. His dark eyes followed my every move, burning my skin and making me even hotter as I kicked my underwear aside.

As my thongs fell, so did the last of my restraints as I approached Maddox, hips swinging, feeling my heart about to explode as my body filled with heat and arousal.

For the first time, Zaeden was so silent, for the first time I had control and could do whatever I wanted with him and that made me feel wild.

I sit on his lap, pressing his cock against my wet entrance as I kissed him again, our tongues dancing as one and I winced in both pain and need. It's pathetic to know how painfully much I need this man.

I rubbed against him, earning moan after moan from both his, while his hands gripped my ass as if his life depended on it.

"Lil cat " the nickname rolled from his lips like a whisper as our lips touched but we didn't kiss "I need to be inside you now"

"Where are your manners, Mr. Carter?" I asked innocently, rubbing myself into him once more earning another groan "Say please first"

"Please" he didn't even hesitate before saying it so desperately, his voice full of need, squeezing my ass in his hands leaving marks on my skin. I bet they look beautiful.

"That's more like it" I muttered with approval, lifting myself enough to slide down his length.

The moment every inch of him filled me and there was nothing left between us we both moaned in unison. I'm so full of him, I feel so alive in his arms. He is so deep inside me, so damn good.

"Ahh, fuckk " he cursed leaning his head back on the sofa, closing his eyes and I couldn't still believe how beautiful his face was "Please" his words came out like begging from his mouth as he was lost in his world. As he was lost in me.

"Please what?" I rolled my pelvis with his fully inside me, hitting the right spot and I cried out. He was stretching me so well, I needed so little and I would collapse in his arms.

"Please ride me" his voice was deep, his eyes tired, begging "Fucking ride my cock"

My pussy reacted immediately to his voice and I bit my lip to hold back another moan. I love this man so much, I might come with just his voice.

"When you ask so nicely" I smiled before shutting him up with a kiss and doing as he said. I rode his cock, fast and wild, losing myself in the rhythm and our moans that filled the room.

At this point, I was glad we were alone because I wouldn't want anyone walking in and seeing me riding Zaeden while he was groaning my name. His hands held my ass, helping me move faster on him, and I used his chest for support to slide up and down on him.

I fuck him, chasing my orgasm. Zaeden drags his tongue up the slide of my neck, making me bite down on my lip while a moan escapes from my mouth. I could feel his cock harden inside me, he was close and so was I.

I knew he wouldn't last long after his cock was in my mouth. I loved knowing I have this power over him, just as much as he has over me.

It took me a few more moves, his cock slamming deep into me, for me to fall apart in his arms moaning his name. My whole body shaking up, clenching around his cock as I cried out. He held me, helping me through an orgasm that clouded my mind.

"I want you to come in my mouth" I whispered against his lips, and he remained speechless. I don't know where I got the courage to talk like that, but I liked it. I felt powerful and wild to see him with a mouth hung open. But it didn't last long before he lazily grin at me slapping me on the ass.

"Then you better get on your knees baby, 'cause I'm about to come" he mumbled in a husky voice, dragging his tongue across his mouth, and I didn't wait for a second invitation.

I slid out of him, kneeling in front of him and taking his cock into my mouth, earning another guttural moan from him as I worked him into my mouth.

Not long after, he exploded in my mouth, his liquid pouring down my throat and I swallowed every drop. There's something so intimate about watching him fall apart in my arms as he cum with his head thrown back, his whole body tight and moaning my name.

His breathing was still heavy and when he calmed down from his orgasm he looked down at me with lazy eyes. I felt a drop of his sperm running down my lips, I collected it with my finger licking it while holding eye contact, and he chuckled shaking his head.

"You'll be the death of me, Lil Cat " he joked, still out of breath, I climbed into his lap, hugging him and he wrapped his arms around my waist. "It would be my pleasure" I smiled before kissing him again. I'm addicted to his lips.

Zaeden then picked me up in his arms, carrying me toward the bed where we just lay there in each other's arms. He was okay, his mind was at ease and he was smiling and talking like he usually does. I barely hold back my grin from this victory.

I had won this battle of myself, with my demons and now I was free from everything.

_____

A couple who found their solace, solitary in each other now would paint their own story.

34. Future

L ily Rose

A year had passed since the night on the balcony, and life had settled into a peaceful rhythm. Many things have changed in a year, Zaeden and I had bought a cosy home away from prying eyes, a sanctuary where we could build our future.

I had returned to my role as Zaeden's secretary, balancing work with helping Sam and Ken manage the business. Sam was still under training to get into missions. Ken was playing the game and I was playing the game behind screens.

Things got normal, Chris lived with his family and visited us when he had free time. We went on lunch dates with families every month. Zaeden and I got closer and closer and we became inseparable.

Our mornings were filled with quiet moments—Zaeden's laughter over breakfast and his touch's warmth as he kissed me goodbye before heading to the office. Evenings were spent in our garden, where we dreamed of the future and whispered promises under the stars.

Our lives were getting normal, every catfight between us turned into fucking every space in the house. Every little mistake turned into spicy, it was a long journey to get peace and a little sex.

But lately, something has changed. I felt a constant fatigue, a sickness that wouldn't go away. I was feeling dizzy and my back ached a lot. Zaeden noticed, his eyes filled with concern. "Lily," he said one morning, his hand on my forehead, "you're burning up. You need to see a doctor. Come on Let's go today."

I shook my head. " Zaeden you need to go to the office today, you have a meeting today and you need to attend that." The worry gnawing at me. "I'll go today," I promised.

After having breakfast together Zaeden left for the office and I got ready for the hospital. I was feeling a bit conscious about this. I had a feeling that something was wrong with me or that today would be a day of surprises for me.

The hospital was a sterile maze of white walls and antiseptic smells. I sat in the waiting room, my heart pounding. When the doctor finally called me in, I felt a mix of relief and dread.

Dr. Patel, a kind-faced woman with gentle eyes, examined me thoroughly. "Lily," she said, her voice calm, "we need to run some tests."

I nodded, my throat dry. "Is it serious?"

She smiled reassuringly. "Let's find out."

This felt like ages. Every passing minute felt like a nightmare to me. Her hands were working taking notes on every moment of mine. Asking me questions about how lately I've been feeling.

The tests seemed to take forever, each minute stretching into an eternity. Finally, Dr. Patel returned, her expression unreadable. She was sitting behind her computer looking at what might be my test. Her glasses are on her nose.

Her expressions were unreadable and the more she went on my anxiety started gripping in. Her voice boomed making me startled. "Lily," she said, her voice calm and normal which made nerves in relief.

"you're pregnant."

The words hung in the air, surreal and overwhelming. "Pregnant?" I echoed, my hand instinctively moving to my stomach. I looked down at my stomach, a smile on my face as my chest blooms with happiness. This was surreal more to be known at exact.

She nodded. "About three weeks along. Congratulations."

A rush of emotions flooded me—joy, fear, excitement, and uncertainty. "Thank you," I whispered, my mind racing. I stood up took the report and walked out of the hospital.

My mind was flooding with emotions and thoughts, How would Zaeden react? Would he be happy? Scared?

I drove the car back to the house, my hand reached out to the drawer where I had my cigarettes kept then the realization broke on me. I threw all the cigarettes out and drove back home.

Back at home, I opened the doors, Zaeden was at home. I was getting ideas about how should I tell him. Do I surprise him? What if he doesn't like it? what if he isn't ready for a child?

I found Zaeden in the garden, his hands dirty from planting new flowers. He looked up, his eyes lighting up when he saw me. "Hey, Lil cat," he said, wiping his hands on his jeans. "How did it go?" He asks

He must have read my face as his face stretched into concern. " Lily, what's wrong? Did the doctor say something? Show me the reports."

I took a deep breath, my heart pounding. "Zaeden," I began, "I have news."

He straightened, his expression serious. "What is it?" I handed him the report and he took it and read them. My heart was pounding so loud that I might die of a heart attack. He was taking in every letter that came into his eyes.

"I'm pregnant," I said, the words tumbling out in a rush.

For a moment, he didn't look up his eyes were still on the report in his hands. He was silent, his eyes wide with shock. Then, a slow smile spread across his face. "Pregnant?" he repeated, his voice filled with wonder.

I nodded, tears welling up. "Yes."

He crossed the distance between us in two strides, lifting me off the ground and spinning me around. "We're going to have a baby," he said, his voice choked with emotion.

I laughed, the sound mingling with my tears. "Yes, we are." A relief passed through me. He was happy. he looked excited and I can't express it.

"We are having a baby Lily, oh my god I'm so happy I can't even express it." He says while palming my cheeks. I giggle as he screams that I'm carrying his child. A sigh leaves my lips.

"I don't know Zaeden If I can be a good mom. I had to kill my mother just to prove my loyalty and for the sake of my brother, I never had my mother's love on my head I just saw guns, knives and bodies. Do you think I'm qualified to be a mother? " I say my voice cracking.

His forehead attaches to mine as he replies. " You were able to love me, tolerate me enough. You passed your legacy to Sam but you still care and you don't let him go on missions. Why don't you think you aren't qualified enough? "

A tear passes down my eyes but Zaeden kisses it away. " You're going to be the best mother In the world and I promise you that. Our child is going to love you the most and I'm here, I'll always be there for you," he says and attaches his lips with me.

The kiss is slow and passionate as our tongue collides. His hands move to my stomach where our little bean is growing. His hands caress my stomach and somehow it brings butterflies to my heart.

" You are not alone Lily, we are going through this journey of life together. " I could only nod at his words. " You are now bound to me Lily, you can't escape me now or never." I smile at him.

We called Sam and Ken to share the news. Sam's voice crackled with excitement over the phone. "Lily, that's amazing! I'm going to be an uncle!"

Ken, ever the practical one, asked, "Do you need anything? How can I help?"

"Just be there," I said, my heart full. "That's all I need."

I then called Chris and his family to share the news. " Oh my fucking gosh Lily for god's sake you're pregnant this can't be better than anything."

Then Mom's face appears. " Congratulations dear We are so happy for you and Zaeden. I hope you guys are the best and when you get time come and meet me." I nod and then hang up.

Arms come into my view as Zaeden wraps his arm behind me. " We are gonna have a beautiful life together, Me, you and the Baby. You're the best thing that happened to me and I'm so proud that I met you at the club."

My head leans on his shoulder as we watch the stars in the sky. "I love you Zaeden. "

"I love you too Lily."

And so, under the watchful gaze of the stars, we embraced the future—ready to face whatever came our way, hand in hand.

———————————

So, as the story continues their life bounds together and creates a new meaning for the future.

35.Until

Z aeden Carter

    Three months had passed since we first learned about the baby, and life had settled into a beautiful, chaotic rhythm. Our home, nestled away from the world's prying eyes, had become a sanctuary of love and laughter. Every morning, I woke to the sound of birdsong and the warmth of Lily's embrace. Her baby bump had grown noticeably larger than expected for three months, filling me with excitement and curiosity.

Our mornings were filled with playful banter and stolen kisses. Today was no different. I found Lily in the kitchen, her hair tousled and a mischievous smile playing on her lips. "Good morning, beautiful," I said, wrapping my arms around her from behind.

She leaned into me, her laughter like music. "Good morning, Zaeden. Ready for another day of being kicked out of the house?"

I chuckled. "You know I just want to stay and care for you."

"And you know I can take care of myself," she replied, turning to kiss me. "Besides, Sam and Ken need you at the office today because I can't go to the warehouse so, you need to go."

Reluctantly, I let her go. "Fine, but only because you insist."

"Maybe you could come home early after the warehouse because you don't have any other meetings to attend." She says as a smirk plasters on her face.

"I can't wait for this day to end early so, I can return to my babies." I go close to her as she peers at me. I smile at her and bring my face close to hers as our lips collide perfectly. Our tongues move perfectly sinking into each other.

After a few seconds, we broke up as she looked at me biting her lip. A smirk draws on my lip as I get to know her intention. " You're horny, aren't you lil cat? " Her smile gets bigger as she licks my earlobe and says, "Don't you have work Mr Carter? "she whispers seductively.

A groan passes my lips as she pushes me back and waves me to go. Giving her a last kiss I leave the house.

Lily worked from home, balancing her responsibilities with helping Sam and Ken manage the family business. She was a force of nature, handling everything with grace and determination. I admired her strength, even as I worried about her overworking herself.

After having a shit of hours at the warehouse I'm back at the house and hear the TV in the background and someone singing and of course, It was my baby dancing slowly syncing to the song. I enter as she smiles at me and waves me to join her.

My steps are slow yet certain she peers at me with her lashes. Her hand comes forward, latching my fingers with her small one. She dances with me keeping her hand protectively around the bump.

This moment felt surreal as the music changed on its own and our legs moved accordingly with the pace. Our gaze locked with each other as a light smile played on our lips. After a few moments, Lily says, "We have an appointment."

After having a shower I got ready as Lily was already ready and was taking files for the appointment.

Today was special. We had an appointment with the doctor for the gender reveal and to listen to the baby's heartbeat for the first time. I couldn't contain my excitement as we drove to the hospital, my hand resting protectively on Lily's growing bump.

The hospital was a familiar place now, but today it felt different. There was an air of anticipation as we sat in the waiting room, our fingers intertwined. Dr. Patel greeted us with a warm smile. "Lily, Zaeden, it's good to see you both. Come in."

"Likewise, Doctor," I said, my voice tinged with nervous excitement.

Dr Patel led us to the examination room, where Lily lay down on the table. The ultrasound machine hummed to life, and I held my breath as the screen flickered.

She took out some gel and applied it to her bare belly and took the machine scanning it on her belly while looking at the screen.

"Let's see what we have here," Dr. Patel said, her eyes focused on the monitor. The room was silent except for the rhythmic beeping of the machine.

And then, we heard it-the steady, rapid heartbeat of our baby. Tears filled my eyes as I squeezed Lily's hand. "That's our baby," I whispered, my voice choked with emotion.

Dr. Patel's smile widened. "That's one of your babies."

Lily and I exchanged confused glances. "One of?" Lily asked, her voice trembling.

Dr. Patel nodded. "Congratulations, you're having twins."

She moved the machine toward us where we saw our babies, we couldn't figure it out until Dr. Patel showed us the twin babies.

The room seemed to spin as the news sank in. Twins. Two heartbeats. Two lives growing inside Lily. I felt a surge of joy and fear all at once. "Twins," I repeated, my voice barely a whisper.

Then she gave us the file where the pictures of our unborn baby were. The tension could be felt in the room as the doctor talked but we both knew that this was not expected.

The doctor gave us instructions for her health and diet as she had to take extra care of herself as she was carrying two babies inside her.

Then we left the hospital together without uttering a word to each other.

Lily Rose

'Twins'. The doctor had said that I was carrying two babies inside of me. Two babies were growing inside of me.

I sat in the passenger seat, my eyes darting towards Zaeden every few seconds. The silence between us was thick, almost suffocating. Zaeden's hands gripped the steering wheel tightly, his knuckles white against the dark leather. He hadn't said a word since we left the hospital, his focus entirely on the road ahead.

My mind raced with a thousand thoughts, each one more troubling than the last. What had the doctor said that could have caused this shift in him? Was it something about the baby? Or was it something about me? I placed a protective hand on my belly bump, feeling the slight flutter of movement beneath my palm. The sensation was usually comforting, but now it only heightened my anxiety.

I glanced at Zaeden again, hoping for some sign, some indication that he was still there with me, but his expression remained unreadable. The man who usually held my hand, whispered reassurances, and made me feel safe was now a stranger, lost in his world. The distance between us felt like a chasm, and I didn't know how to bridge it.

"Zaeden," I finally whispered, my voice trembling. But he didn't respond, his eyes never leaving the road. The silence stretched on, and my heart ached with worry. I could only hope that whatever was troubling him, we could face it together. But for now, all I could do was hold on to my bump and pray for the best.

The car's engine hummed softly, a stark contrast to the storm brewing inside me. I tried to recall the doctor's words, searching for any clue that might explain Zaeden's behaviour. My thoughts spiralled into dark corners, imagining worst-case scenarios. Tears pricked at the corners of my eyes, but I blinked them away, refusing to let fear take over.

My fingers tightened around my belly, as if by holding on I could protect my unborn child from whatever unknown threat loomed ahead. I took a deep breath, trying to steady my racing heart. "Zaeden, please," I said, my voice barely above a whisper. "Talk to me."

Still, there was no response. The silence was deafening, each second stretching into an eternity. My mind was a whirlwind of emotions-fear, confusion, and a deep, gnawing worry. I needed to know what was going on, needed to understand why the man I loved was shutting me out. But for now, all I could do was wait and hope that the answers would come soon.

The drive felt endless, each minute stretching into an eternity. My mind was a battlefield of emotions, each thought more unsettling than the last. I couldn't shake the feeling that something was wrong. The doctor's words echoed in my mind, but they were a blur, overshadowed by Zaeden's uncharacteristic silence.

Zaeden turned onto a road that I didn't recognize, the unfamiliar scenery making my heart race. "Zaeden, where are we going?" I asked, my voice tinged with anxiety. But he remained silent, his eyes fixed on the road ahead. The trees blurred past us, their shadows casting eerie patterns on the car's interior.

My unease grew with each passing moment. The road seemed to stretch endlessly, and the further we went, the more isolated I felt. "Zaeden, please, talk to me," I pleaded, but he didn't respond. The silence was deafening, amplifying my fears. I clutched my belly bump protectively, feeling the baby move slightly as if sensing my distress.

Suddenly, the car came to an abrupt stop. I looked around, realizing we were in the middle of a dense forest. The place felt eerily familiar, and a wave of memories washed over me. This was the forest where Zaeden had taken me on one of our first dates, a place that had brought us closer together. It was also where we had reunited after a long separation.

Zaeden got out of the car and walked around to my side, opening the door for me. I stepped out, still holding my bump protectively. The forest was quiet, the only sounds being the rustling of leaves and the distant call of birds. Zaeden took my hand, his grip firm yet gentle, and without a word, he led me into the forest.

As we walked, the memories of our time here flooded back. The laughter, the shared secrets, the promises we had made to each other. Despite my anxiety, I felt a small spark of hope. Maybe he had brought me here to remind us of those moments, to find solace in a place that had once meant so much to us.

We walked deeper into the forest, the path becoming more familiar with each step. Finally, we reached a small clearing, the same spot where we had once sat and talked for hours. Zaeden stopped and turned to face me, his eyes filled with a mix of emotions.

"Lily," he began, his voice soft but steady. "I brought you here because I needed to remind myself of what we have, of what we're fighting for."

Tears welled up in my eyes as I looked at him. "Zaeden, whatever it is, we can face it together," I said, my voice trembling. "Just tell me what's going on."

He took a deep breath, his eyes never leaving mine. "The doctor said there might be complications," he admitted, his voice breaking. "But I needed to come here, to remember that no matter what happens, we have each other."

I squeezed his hand, feeling a sense of determination wash over me. "We'll get through this," I said firmly. "Together."

We walked until we saw the edge of the mountains. This was our place, our solitude, our peace. Where our story has started and always gave a new meaning to our lives.

As we stood in the clearing, a nagging feeling tugged at the back of my mind. Something about Zaeden's demeanour suggested there was more to this visit than just a reminder of our past. I watched him closely, searching for any clues in his expression. His eyes held a depth of emotion that I couldn't quite decipher.

Before I could voice my thoughts, Zaeden suddenly dropped to one knee, pulling a small box from his pocket. My breath caught in my throat as he looked up at me, his eyes filled with a mixture of love and determination.

"Lily," he began, his voice steady but filled with emotion. "From the moment I met you, you've been my rock, my confidant, and my greatest love. We've faced so much together, and I can't imagine my life without you by my side."

Tears welled up in my eyes as his words washed over me. They weren't just words; they were a testament to everything we had been through, every challenge we had overcome together.

Zaeden opened the box, revealing a simple yet elegant ring. It was exactly the kind of ring I had always loved-no big diamonds, just a beautiful, understated design that spoke volumes. My heart swelled with emotion as I looked at it, and then back at him.

"I know this isn't the most traditional moment," he continued, his voice softening. "But I wanted to do this here, in the place that means so much to both of us. Lily, will you marry me?"

For a moment, I was speechless, overwhelmed by the depth of his love and the significance of this moment. I felt the baby move again as if sharing in our joy. I nodded, tears streaming down my face. "Yes, Zaeden," I whispered, my voice choked with emotion. "Yes, a thousand times yes."

He slipped the ring onto my finger, and I felt a surge of happiness and relief. As we stood there, wrapped in each other's arms, a rustling sound came from the bushes nearby. I pulled back slightly, glancing around in confusion.

Before I could say anything, Chris, Sam, and Chris's mom and dad suddenly emerged from the underbrush, looking slightly dishevelled but grinning from ear to ear.

"Surprise!" Chris shouted, throwing his arms up in the air. "We couldn't let you have this moment all to yourselves!"

Sam laughed, brushing leaves off his shirt. "Yeah, we figured you might need some moral support," he added with a wink.

Chris's mom stepped forward, her eyes twinkling with amusement. "We were hiding in the bushes the whole time," she confessed, her voice filled with laughter. "We didn't want to miss this special moment."

Chris's dad nodded, a proud smile on his face. "Zaeden told us his plan, and we just had to be here to see it through."

I couldn't help but laugh, the tension of the past few hours melting away in the presence of our friends and family. "You guys are unbelievable," I said, shaking my head in disbelief. "But thank you. This means so much to us."

Zaeden chuckled, wrapping an arm around my shoulders. "I wanted to make sure we had our loved ones here to share this moment," he said, his eyes shining with happiness.

Chris grinned, pulling out his phone. "Alright, everyone, group photo time!" he announced, gathering us all together. "Say 'engagement!'"

"Engagement!" we all chorused, laughing as the camera clicked. At that moment, surrounded by the people we loved, I felt a sense of joy and contentment that I knew would carry us through whatever challenges lay ahead.

As the laughter died down, Chris's mom stepped forward, her eyes misty with emotion. "Lily, Zaeden, we are so happy for you both," she said, her voice trembling slightly. "This is just the beginning of a beautiful journey, and we are honoured to be a part of it."

Sam nodded, his usual playful demeanour replaced by a rare seriousness. "You two are perfect for each other," he said, his voice sincere. "And I know that whatever comes your way, you'll face it together."

Chris's dad clapped Zaeden on the back, a proud smile on his face. "You've got a good one here, son," he said, looking at me. "Take care of each other."

Zaeden squeezed my hand, his eyes filled with love. "We will," he promised, his voice steady. "We always will."

"Okay everyone we have to announce everyone." I looked at Zaeden as he smiled standing beside me, his hands on my lower waist rubbing slowly to ease the back pain.

"We're having twins," I echoed, my voice filled with wonder.

Everyone gasped but the smile was replaced by it. "Are you serious?" Chris asked as Sam smiled. I nodded as words couldn't form on my lips. "I'm going to be the uncle of twins this is so exciting," Chris said as Sam came beside me.

I found a quiet moment to sit with Sam. He had always been my rock, my confidant, and seeing him here, sharing in this special moment, meant the world to me.

Sam nudged me gently, a playful smile on his face. "So, how does it feel to be engaged, Li?" he asked, his eyes twinkling with genuine happiness.

I smiled, feeling a warmth spread through me. "It's surreal, Sam. I never imagined it would happen like this, but it's perfect," I said, glancing down at the ring on my finger. "Zaeden surprised me."

Sam chuckled, shaking his head. "He did good. I have to admit, I was a bit sceptical when he told me his plan, but seeing you two together... it just feels right."

I looked at him, my heart swelling with gratitude. "Thank you for being here, Sam. It means so much to me."

He shrugged, but I could see the emotion in his eyes. "Of course, Li. You're my sister. I wouldn't miss this for the world." He paused, his expression turning serious. "How are you feeling about everything? I know it's been a lot to take in."

I took a deep breath, considering his question. "It's been overwhelming, but in a good way. I was so worried earlier, with Zaeden acting strange and the doctor's news. But now, I feel hopeful. I know we can face whatever comes our way."

Sam nodded, his gaze softening. "I'm happy for you, Lily. You deserve all the happiness in the world. And Zaeden... he's a good guy. I'm glad you found each other."

I felt tears prick at the corners of my eyes, but I blinked them away, smiling at my brother. "Thanks, Sam. That means a lot coming from you."

He grinned, pulling me into a hug. "Just promise me one thing," he said, his voice muffled against my shoulder.

"Anything," I replied, hugging him back.

"Promise me you'll let me be the cool uncle," he said, pulling back to look at me with a mischievous glint in his eye. "I want to spoil my niece or nephew rotten."

I laughed, feeling a weight lift off my shoulders. "Deal," I said, wiping away a tear. "But only if you promise to be the best uncle ever."

"Done and done," Sam said, giving me a mock salute. "Now, let's get back to the party. We've got a lot to celebrate."

"Lily, I need you to know something. You've always been the strong one, the one who held everything together. Seeing you happy, seeing you with Zaeden... it means everything to me. I know things haven't always been easy, but you deserve this. You deserve all the love and happiness in the world."

Tears welled up in my eyes, and I couldn't hold them back this time. "Sam, you've always been there for me, through everything. I don't know what I would have done without you. Your support means more to me than I can ever say."

He hugged me tightly, his voice thick with emotion. "We'll always have each other's backs, Lily. No matter what. And now, you have Zaeden too. You're not alone."

I nodded, feeling a profound sense of gratitude and love. "Thank you, Sam. For everything."

As the sun began to set, casting a golden glow over the clearing, we all sat down on the grass, sharing stories and laughter. The worries that had plagued me earlier seemed distant now, replaced by a sense of peace and hope. Surrounded by our friends and family, I knew that we could face anything together.

Chris, ever the entertainer, started recounting a hilarious story from his college days, complete with exaggerated gestures and sound effects. We all laughed until our sides hurt, the sound echoing through the forest. It felt like a celebration, not just of our engagement, but of the love and support that bound us all together.

As the evening wore on, Zaeden and I stole a moment alone, walking a little further into the forest. The memories of our past visits here filled the air, each step a reminder of how far we had come. Zaeden stopped and turned to me, his eyes reflecting the fading light.

"Lily," he said softly, taking both my hands in his. "I know things have been tough, and there are still challenges ahead. But I want you to know that I am here for you, always. This ring is a symbol of my love and commitment to you, and our future together."

I felt tears welling up again, but this time they were tears of joy. "Zaeden, I love you more than words can express," I said, my voice trembling. "And I promise to stand by you, through every joy and every sorrow. You are my home, my heart, and my forever."

We kissed, a gentle promise of the life we would build together. As we walked back to join our friends and family, hand in hand, I felt a renewed sense of hope and determination. Whatever lay ahead, we would face it together, bound by an unbreakable love.

As we rejoined the group, I felt a renewed sense of joy and gratitude. Surrounded by the people I loved, I knew that whatever challenges lay ahead, we would face them together, with love, laughter, and a little bit of mischief.

As we all gathered for one last photo, the laughter and joy in the air were palpable. This moment, filled with love, hope, and a little bit of mischief, was a testament to the bonds that held us together. And as the camera clicked, capturing our smiles and the light in our eyes, I knew that this was just the beginning of a beautiful journey.

Together, we would face every joy and every sorrow, every challenge and every triumph. And with each step, we would be guided by the love that had brought us here, to this place, to this moment.

Here's to the future, to love, and to the unbreakable bonds that make life truly extraordinary.

Elysian - Relating to or characteristic of heaven or paradise.

Epilogue

- -

L ily Carter

Two years have passed since that unforgettable day in the forest, and life has been a whirlwind of joy, challenges, and beautiful moments. Zaeden and I got married in a simple, intimate ceremony surrounded by our closest friends and family. The day was perfect, filled with laughter, love, and the promise of a future together.

Now, as I sit in our cosy living room, I watch our two children playing on the floor. Our daughter, Emma, with her bright eyes and infectious giggle, is the spitting image of me but has inherited Zaeden's mischievous personality. She's always up to something, whether it's hiding her toys in the most unexpected places or trying to sneak an extra cookie when she thinks no one is looking. Her laughter fills the house, a constant reminder of the joy she brings into our lives.

Our son, Ethan, on the other hand, looks just like Zaeden with his dark hair and intense gaze, but he has a calm and thoughtful nature. He's the one who carefully arranges his toys in neat rows, who sits quietly with a book, lost in his little world. Yet, there's a spark of curiosity in his eyes that mirrors my own, a thirst for knowledge and understanding.

Zaeden walks in, carrying a tray with two steaming cups of tea. He sets it down on the table and sits beside me, wrapping an arm around my shoulders. "How are our little troublemakers doing?" he asks, his eyes twinkling with affection.

I smile, leaning into him. "They're perfect, just like their father," I say, watching as Emma tries to stack blocks while Ethan knocks them over, both of them dissolving into fits of giggles.

Zaeden chuckles, pressing a kiss to my temple. "And just like their mother, full of love and determination."

Suddenly, Emma decides it's time for a game of hide-and-seek. She grabs Ethan's hand and they both dash off, their laughter echoing through the house. Zaeden and I exchange a knowing look, and with a playful grin, we join in the chase. We find them hiding behind the curtains, their giggles giving them away. Zaeden swoops in, scooping Emma up into his arms while I catch Ethan, tickling him until he's breathless with laughter.

"Gotcha!" Zaeden exclaims, spinning Emma around. She squeals with delight, her eyes sparkling with mischief.

Ethan, still catching his breath, looks up at me with a wide grin. "Mommy, can we play again?" he asks, his voice filled with excitement.

I laugh, ruffling his hair. "Of course, sweetheart. But this time, you have to count."

As we play, the house is filled with the sounds of laughter and joy. The worries and challenges of the past seem distant now, replaced by the simple, beautiful moments we share as a family. Zaeden and I steal glances at each other, our hearts full of love and gratitude for the life we've built together.

Our wedding was a simple affair, just as we had always wanted. Surrounded by the people who mattered most, we exchanged vows under a canopy of twinkling lights. Sam walked me down the aisle, his eyes filled with pride and love. Chris and his family were there, along with our closest friends, all of them cheering us on as we took this next step in our journey.

Amidst the chaos and love, I had been working on a special project—a secret room for our children, a gift they would discover when they were older.

The room was tucked away in the attic, accessible only through a small, hidden door. Inside, I had created a cosy space filled with soft cushions, fairy lights, and shelves lined with their favourite books and toys. But the most special part of the room was the wall where I had been pasting pictures of Emma and Ethan, capturing their sweetest, funniest, and most embarrassing moments.

Today, I had just taken a new picture of Emma and Ethan covered in flour after an impromptu baking session that had turned into a flour fight. Their faces were lit up with laughter, and I couldn't wait to add this memory to the wall.

I climbed the narrow stairs to the attic, the picture clutched in my hand. Unlocking the small door, I stepped inside the secret room. The fairy lights cast a warm glow, and the walls were already adorned with countless photos. There was Emma's first birthday, her face smeared with cake; Ethan's first steps, his expression a mix of determination and surprise; and countless other moments that made my heart swell with love.

I found an empty spot on the wall and carefully pasted the new picture. Stepping back, I admired the collage of memories, each one a testament to the joy and love that filled our lives.

Just then, I heard the creak of the attic stairs. Turning around, I saw Zaeden standing in the doorway, a curious smile on his face. "What are you up to, Lily?" he asked, stepping into the room.

I smiled, feeling a mix of excitement and nervousness. "I was just adding a new picture to the wall," I said, gesturing to the collage. "This is my secret project for Emma and Ethan. I want them to have a place where they can see all the wonderful moments of their childhood when they're older."

Zaeden walked over to the wall, his eyes scanning the photos. "This is amazing," he said softly, his voice filled with admiration. "You've captured so many beautiful moments."

I nodded, feeling a lump in my throat. "I want them to know how much they are loved, how much joy they bring into our lives," I said, my voice trembling slightly. "And I want them to have a place where they can come and remember all the happy times."

Zaeden wrapped his arms around me, pulling me close. "They are going to love this," he said, his voice filled with certainty. "And so do I. This is a beautiful gift, Lily."

I leaned into him, feeling a sense of peace and contentment. "Thank you, Zaeden," I whispered. "For everything."

As we stood there, surrounded by the memories of our children's laughter and love, I knew that this secret room would be a cherished part of their lives. It was a testament to the unbreakable bond that held our family together, a reminder of the joy and love that filled our home. As the years passed, I would continue to add to the wall, capturing every sweet, funny, and embarrassing moment, creating a tapestry of memories that would last a lifetime.

As the sun began to set, casting a warm golden glow through the windows, I couldn't help but reflect on how much our lives had changed in the past two years. The house was filled with the sounds of our children's laughter, a melody that never failed to bring a smile to my face. Emma and Ethan were now playing a game of tag, their little feet pattering across the wooden floor.

Zaeden and I sat on the couch, watching them with a mixture of amusement and pride. "They're growing up so fast," I said, leaning my head on his shoulder.

He nodded, his eyes never leaving the children. "They are. And they're becoming more like us every day," he said with a chuckle. "Emma with her mischievous streak and Ethan with his thoughtful nature."

I smiled, thinking about how perfectly our children embodied the best parts of us. "It's amazing to see bits of ourselves in them," I said softly. "And to think about all the adventures we still have ahead of us."

Just then, Emma ran over to us, her cheeks flushed with excitement. "Mommy, Daddy, come play with us!" she exclaimed, grabbing Zaeden's hand and tugging him off the couch.

Ethan followed, his eyes bright with anticipation. "Yeah, come on! We need more players for our game."

Zaeden and I exchanged a glance, both of us grinning. "Alright, you two," Zaeden said, standing up and stretching. "But be warned, your mom and I are pretty good at this game."

I laughed, getting up and joining them. "Let's see if you can keep up with us," I teased, ruffling Ethan's hair.

The next hour was filled with laughter and playful competition as we chased each other around the house. Emma's giggles were infectious, and Ethan's determination to win was endearing. Zaeden and I played along, letting ourselves be caught and then turning the tables on the kids. It was moments like these that made all the challenges worth it.

Eventually, we all collapsed onto the living room floor, breathless and happy. Emma snuggled up to Zaeden, her eyelids drooping with exhaustion, while Ethan rested his head on my lap, his little hand clutching mine.

Zaeden looked over at me, his eyes filled with love. "This is what it's all about, isn't it?" he said softly. "These moments, this family."

I nodded, feeling a lump in my throat. "Yes, it is," I whispered. "I wouldn't trade it for anything in the world."

As the evening turned into night, we carried the kids to their beds, tucking them in with gentle kisses and whispered goodnights. Zaeden and I stood in the doorway, watching them sleep, their faces peaceful and content.

Later that evening, after the children were tucked into bed and the house had settled into a peaceful quiet, Zaeden and I found ourselves alone in the living room. The soft glow of the fireplace cast a warm light, creating a cosy atmosphere. We sat together on the couch, a comfortable silence enveloping us.

Zaeden reached for my hand, intertwining his fingers with mine. "It's hard to believe how far we've come," he said softly, his eyes reflecting the flickering flames.

I nodded, leaning my head on his shoulder. "It feels like just yesterday we were standing in that forest, unsure of what the future held," I replied, my voice filled with nostalgia.

He smiled a hint of amusement in his eyes. "We've faced so many storms together, haven't we? From the uncertainty of our first doctor's visit to the sleepless nights with Emma and Ethan."

I laughed softly, remembering those early days. "I don't think I've ever been so exhausted in my life," I admitted. "But every moment was worth it."

Zaeden's expression turned serious, his gaze locking onto mine. "Lily, I want you to know how much I appreciate everything you've done for our family. You've been my rock, my constant source of strength. I couldn't have asked for a better partner."

Tears welled up in my eyes, and I squeezed his hand. "And you, Zaeden, have been my anchor. You've always been there, even when things were tough. I couldn't have done this without you."

He leaned in, pressing a gentle kiss to my forehead. "We've built something beautiful together," he said, his voice filled with emotion. "And I wouldn't trade any of it for the world."

I smiled, feeling a deep sense of contentment. "We've had our share of challenges, but we've also had so many wonderful moments. Watching Emma and Ethan grow, seeing their personalities develop... it's been incredible."

Zaeden nodded, his eyes softening. "They've brought so much joy into our lives. And seeing you with them, seeing the love and care you give them, it makes me fall in love with you all over again."

I felt a tear slip down my cheek, and I wiped it away, laughing softly. "You're going to make me cry," I said, my voice trembling with emotion.

He pulled me closer, wrapping his arms around me. "Let it out, Lily. We've been through so much, and we've come out stronger on the other side."

We sat there for a while, holding each other, reflecting on our journey. The storms we had weathered together had only strengthened our bond, and the love we shared had grown deeper with each passing day.

As the fire crackled softly, I felt a profound sense of peace. Our journey was far from over, but with Zaeden by my side, I knew we could face anything. Together, we had built a life filled with love, laughter, and countless beautiful moments. And I couldn't wait to see what the future held for us.

"Here's to us," I whispered, lifting my head to look into Zaeden's eyes. "To our past, our present, and our future."

"To us," he echoed, his voice filled with love and determination. "Always and forever."

As I closed my eyes, I felt a deep sense of peace and gratitude. Our journey was far from over, but with Zaeden by my side and our children filling our lives with joy, I knew we could face anything. Here's to the future, to the adventures that await, and to the unbreakable bond that holds us all together. Our story is just beginning, and I can't wait to see where it takes us next.

———————————

Until next time!